BEYOND WORDS

THE HUTTON FAMILY BOOK 1

ABBY BROOKS

For my Mr. Wonderful. Our life is a dream, punctuated by moments of perfect harmony. Thank you for loving me.

Connect with
ABBY BROOKS

WEBSITE:
www.abbybrooksfiction.com

FACEBOOK:
http://www.facebook.com/abbybrooksauthor

FACEBOOK FAN GROUP:
https://www.facebook.com/
groups/AbbyBrooksBooks/

TWITTER:
http://www.twitter.com/xo_abbybrooks

INSTAGRAM:
http://www.instagram.com/xo_abbybrooks

BOOK+MAIN BITES:
https://bookandmainbites.com/abbybrooks

Want to be one of the first to know about new releases, get exclusive content, and exciting giveaways? Sign up for my newsletter on my website:

www.abbybrooksfiction.com

And, as always, feel free to send me an email at: abby@abbybrooksfiction.com

Books by

ABBY BROOKS

Brookside Romance

Wounded

Inevitably You

This Is Why

Along Comes Trouble

Come Home To Me

Wilde Boys Series with Will Wright

Taking What Is Mine

Claiming What Is Mine

Protecting What Is Mine

The Moore Family Series

Blown Away (Ian and Juliet)

Carried Away (James and Ellie)

Swept Away (Harry and Willow)

Break Away (Lilah and Cole)

Purely Wicked (Ashley & Jackson)

Love Is...

Love Is Crazy (Dakota & Dominic)

Love Is Beautiful (Chelsea & Max)

Love Is Everything (Maya & Hudson)

Immortal Memories

Immortal Memories Part 1

Immortal Memories Part 2

As Wren Williams

Bad, Bad Prince

Woodsman

CHAPTER ONE

Cat

Dearest Journal,

Day 431... and the search continues.

WHERE IN THE WORLD HAS MY ORGASM GONE?? You know better than anyone I've looked everywhere. Under the bed. In the fridge. I even cleaned out the trunk of my car (just in case). Nash sure seems to find his without any problem. So, why in the name of all that's holy has mine gone M.I.A.?

At this point I'm beginning to wonder if it's my fault. Was it something I said? Please, if you'll just come back, we can talk it out. I know we can. Please come back! Pretty please?

If I wasn't in a public place right now, I'd laugh.

On second thought, maybe I'd cry.

Nah, I definitely think I'll stick with laughter. There's too much real tragedy in the world for me to look at something like this as anything but a joke.

On paper, Nash and I are good together. We've been good together and we'll continue being good together. For the rest of our years. This is just a little bump in the road. He's overworked and I'm...what? What am I?

Bored?

Uninspired?

Those are big words for someone like me, even though I know I'm the one who wrote them. Someone with so much going for her she can't help but breathe it in and sit back in quiet awe.

But still...

I miss the way it feels to lose myself. That molten feeling that starts low. A thrum. A throb. Then it begins to work its way through my body and next thing you know I'm panting and screaming and lost in bliss and...

...I don't know what else.

It says something that I can no longer find the words to describe it properly. That it's been so long I don't even remember how it feels.

I miss feeling beautiful.

I miss feeling passion.

I miss *feeling*.

I need to feel like a woman made of fire and energy and possibility again. Not this empty body, filled with gray and ash and boredom. I miss that surge of adrenaline that used to spin and twist through my stomach when Nash looked at me. A tornado of love, setting my nerve-endings on fire.

For that matter, I miss having Nash look at me, but that's another thing altogether. He's so busy with work and I respect that he's building our future, but I sure as hell am bored in the present.

He's tired, I get it, but one smack on my ass and I'm supposed to be ready to go? He climbs on. Won't even look me in the eye. No kissing. No touching. No connection. No foreplay at all. It's just, I don't know, clinical. A means to an end.

My body is a tool, designed for his pleasure and his pleasure alone. And really, I wonder if he even gets anything out of it. I mean, he definitely finishes, so there's that.

But there's more to sex than just the physical side of things, right? I know men and women are different, but there has to be more than a muscle spasm and some fluid and we're set. Right? I mean, *right?* Everything in this world revolves around sex.

Wars have started...

Empires collapsed...

Friends and family walk around with knives firmly lodged in backs...

If it's really all about a second-long dick sneeze, then I'm just ashamed about the human race in general. It *has* to be about the connection. About sharing something that intimate and that special and that personal with someone you love and cherish and adore. There has to be something spiritual to it. There just has to be.

sigh

I stopped believing Nash feels anything but annoyed and obligated to me a long time ago. Although...that's not fair. That's me being melodramatic. He works hard. I know he loves me. Things just fade after that first burst of new love.

We're in the Comfortable Zone now. Capital C. Capital Z.

That's just as good. Better even. I know him and he knows me and we don't need fireworks to remind us we're special to each other.

Although I do miss the fireworks...

And you want to know the real kick in the shins? I can't even get myself off anymore. Believe me, I've tried...

...and tried...

...and tried...

There's just...nothing.

It's like I'm numb.

Dead.

Like all the feeling has been sucked out of my body and I'm just a shell of who I used to be.

See? None of this is Nash's fault, is it? If I can't even do it for myself, it's got to be something with me, not anything to do with our relationship. But honestly, I'm too young to face the rest of my life having to go through the motions of sex without getting anything from it. It's messy. Awkward. Sometimes it hurts.

Please tell me this isn't all I have to look forward to.

Please tell me there's more to life and love than disappointment.

I don't want to spend the rest of my years surrounded by people and still feeling completely alone...

CHAPTER TWO

LUCAS

My feet thumped against the sand as early morning light glittered off the ocean. Sweat dripped down my back and chest and I fought the limp in my left leg for as long as was healthy. A few more steps and I stopped, shaking out my thigh as breath ripped through my lungs. My doctors called the fact that I was running at all nothing short of miraculous, but I was annoyed that my body continued to betray me time and time again. I still had miles left in me, but my damn leg was done.

I raked my hands through my blonde hair and stared out over the water, drowning in deep thoughts. My life wasn't supposed to be like this. I wasn't supposed to be here, drifting and useless. I wasn't

supposed to wake up panting, drenched in sweat, shivering and shaking in fear until I remembered where I
was. I was supposed to be making the world a better
place, not wasting time and taking up space and being
forced to give up long before I was done.

Everything I thought I was or ever would be, died
back in Afghanistan. Every hope. Every dream. Every
plan I had for the future. Before, I had purpose. Since
the incident, I merely existed. Life was little more
than a string of days to get through. Nothing more.
Nothing less. With one last look at the waves rolling
up to the beach, I turned and made my way back to my
car, accepting my pace, walking slowly so as not to
limp.

The docs assured me I wouldn't do any more
damage to my body as long as I listened to the warning
signs. Over the last year, I had learned that pushing
past the pain would leave me in agony for the next
couple days.

So, time and time again, I walked right up to the
pain, stared it in the face, and then turned around and
sent myself home. Some days were better than others.
Some were worse. But on the whole, I lasted longer
than I used to, so I counted it as a win.

As I approached my car, my phone vibrated in my
pocket. I slipped it out and answered a call from my
younger brother as gulls strutted in front of me,

keeping a safe distance and a watchful eye in case I had food to toss their way.

"Hit me with the good stuff, Wy-guy." I yanked open the door and pulled out a towel to swipe over my face.

"I have good stuff, and I have bad stuff. Whatcha want first?"

I ran the towel through my hair and closed my eyes. "Let's get the bad stuff out of the way."

"Alright. Bad stuff it is." Wyatt paused. "Dad passed away last night."

And so, that was that.

I had been waiting years to hear those words. For most of my adult life really. I knew for a fact all five of us Hutton kids wished our father would curl up and die more than once throughout our lives. Despite outward appearances, despite what the community thought about his philanthropy, despite the father he was when we were little, it turned out he wasn't a nice man, after all.

"And the good stuff?" I asked my brother.

Wyatt huffed into the phone. "Dad passed away last night."

I bobbed my head in agreement...understanding... acceptance. The asshole had held on too long as it was. "How's Mom?"

"You know Mom. She's taking it gracefully.

Mourning the loss of the man she fell in love with while celebrating the loss of the man she ended up with."

I never understood why she stayed after things got bad. She said it was for us kids, but that never made sense. Mom was too smart not to see the effect it had on us once Dad started drinking. We scattered to the wind as soon as we could, all of us but Wyatt, who said he stayed to help with the business. What he wouldn't admit, but what everyone knew, was that he stayed to keep Mom safe and sane.

The scattering of the Hutton tribe was so complete, my sister couldn't bring herself to make an appearance when I got hurt. Wyatt, Caleb, and Eli put their heads down and stood in stony silence next to Mom and Dad in the hospital room, but Harlow sent a text and a fruit basket and called it a day.

Wyatt droned on about the funeral arrangements, which would be massive to sate the public's grief. No one understood why most of us Hutton kids left the moment we were able. They called us ungrateful. Self-ish. Spoiled.

If only they knew.

"Mom's calling in the cavalry. It's time to circle the wagons, brother," Wyatt said, pulling me out of my thoughts.

"I expected as much."

There was a pause and then, "I didn't know whether or not to count all of us being together again as good or bad."

"It's probably a little of both," I said, though the thought of seeing my family sans Dad had me smiling. My siblings and I used to be close, before we learned how to duck and cover when Dad was around. When was the last time we were all in the same place at the same time? If Harlow had been there, it would have been when I was in the hospital. But she pulled the no-show, so the last time I could remember all five of us being together was right after I enlisted in the Marines. "Everyone coming?"

"Far as I know." Wyatt coughed, and the faint rustle of shuffling papers sounded in my ear. "Flights are being planned. Armor is being donned. Lines are being drawn."

"You make it sound like getting ready for war."

"Isn't that what happens when all of us come home?"

I closed my eyes and leaned against my car. Living with Dad had turned life into a battlefield. Now that he was gone, I hoped our family could heal. I said as much to Wyatt who snorted, but agreed. As the only one of us to stick around, he knew what Dad was capable of, better than anyone.

"Mom has rooms set aside at the resort, by the way.

You just need to get your bionic ass down here and it'll be like old times."

"My bionic ass, huh?"

"You've got so much metal in that backside, you might as well be Robocop."

I shook my head. Only Wyatt would turn his brother getting blown up in Afghanistan into a joke. He made it sound like I'd lost my leg instead of the pins, rods, and shrapnel embedded in my abdomen, hip, and thigh. I told him as much, but as usual, he didn't seem to care, claiming it was so much more fun looking at things the way he did. We finished our call and I dropped my phone into the cup holder in my car. A gust of wind blew as I pulled my T-shirt over my head and breathed in the salty air.

Dad was gone.

After all these years, after all we'd been through and run from, the news was anticlimactic. The sun still shone. The ocean still roared. The gulls still squawked and circled.

Life still ticked by for the rest of the world, their existence unaffected by our tragedy. While I fought for my life in a hospital bed in Germany, the Pats won the Super Bowl. Fans celebrated. Babies were made. No one but a small circle of people knew or cared about my struggle.

As of last night, my mother's life was shattered, my

siblings and me dropping whatever we had going on to help her figure out how to move forward. While we scrambled, life kept on keeping on for the rest of the world. The realization, while sobering, also freed me from a shit-ton of anxiety. Even the most ground-breaking events of our lives were nothing more than blips on the radar. No matter how hard things seemed while we were living them, we would move past them and find better times. We all carried scars. We just had to learn not to limp.

The thought of going home intrigued me. Some of my best and worst memories lived in the Keys, trapped in the walls of that old house. As much as I liked the thought of seeing Mom, Eli, Caleb, Wyatt, and Harlow again, I wondered how being around them would affect me. How it would affect all of us, really.

Can you survive a war and return to the scene of the bloodiest battles without consequence? I thought of explosions. Of smoke. Of the bodies of friends flying through the air. Of pain spreading like ice and fire in my side, my leg, my hip. I pushed the memories away as I shivered, even as a fresh sheen of sweat broke across my brow.

A car pulled up beside me. The doors opened and teenagers poured out, laughing and joking in their swimsuits and sun-streaked hair. They had so much in front of them. So much to learn. I sent a silent prayer to anyone listening that they learned more about the good than the bad.

As they made their way over the sand, a gull fluttered to the pavement a few feet away, nearly tame after years of being fed scraps. He strutted around, watching me with his shiny black eyes. I dug through my bag and found some old chips to toss his way before unlocking my phone and checking for flights to the Keys.

CHAPTER THREE

CAT

My phone buzzed on the table in a crowded coffee shop, interrupting my journaling tirade about my lost orgasm. I jumped and almost knocked my iced coffee right off the edge. Thankfully, I caught it just before it fell and quietly congratulated myself on my quick reflexes. It had to be a sign. In a string of not so great days, this was sure to be a good one.

Condensation coated my hand and I wiped it on my shorts before snapping my journal shut and answering the call, eyes lighting up at the caller ID. Christopher Magic—obviously not his real name, though he swore it was—the purple-haired bodybuilder who came out of the closet two years ago and pursued his dream of therapeutic massage.

"What's good, Magic Man?" I asked into the phone. His name tickled me, and I used it as frequently as I could. I didn't care if he made it up, it was fun and the world needed more of that.

"Hey, Kitty Cat," he purred in a way that could only mean he wanted my undivided attention for whatever he was about to say. Maybe it wasn't going to be such a good day after all. The only thing Christopher Magic loved more than drama was being the one to drop the bomb. If he was purring, I was in trouble.

I glanced at the time. "It's only eleven. My first client isn't until twelve, right?"

"Oh, sweetie. I don't think you're going to be meeting clients today. Or any day soon, for that matter." The lilt of his voice told me he had dirt to dish and dish it he did.

I listened in shock as Chris explained what he found when he arrived at Utopia, the salon and day spa where we worked. Or rather, where we used to work.

"Closed?" I asked when he finished. "Like, for good?"

"Yes. Like for good. There's nothing here. The door is locked. The lights are off. The place is empty. E. M. P. T. Y. Darla and I are just standing out here like assholes staring at an empty building."

I could imagine the two of them prancing and posturing in the parking lot, pretending to be put out when they were, in fact, thrilled to have something this big to complain about for the next month and a half.

Chris lowered his voice. "Do you think they had ties to the mob?"

I very much doubted they had ties to the mob, but I kept my mouth shut. Chris lived on gossip and his days were fueled by imagination and chaos. My more practical suggestions of tax evasion or...okay. I really didn't have any practical suggestions. There wasn't one down-to-earth reason for an entire salon to up and disappear overnight.

"Well, hell." I gathered my things, laying my journal on the seat next to me as I slipped my pen into my purse and slurped down the rest of my iced coffee.

It wasn't like Utopia was the best place to work. It wasn't the worst, either. What it did have going for it was that it was a steady source of income. Though, according to Nash, I didn't really need an income, steady or not. He earned more than enough money to support the two of us, but there was something important in knowing I contributed. Something Nash—with his 'old money values'—would never understand in the same way he couldn't understand my friendship with Magic Man. No matter how much I explained that Chris was fun, that he did things his way and loved himself for it, Nash only rolled his eyes and changed the subject.

I took the job at Utopia because I wanted to understand life as a masseuse before I took on the challenges of running my own business—which was the ultimate goal, a health and wellness business of my own. Nash countered that I was stalling because I knew massage therapy was a terrible way to make a living.

He couldn't have been more wrong.

Being a small business owner sounded all hunky-dory and filled to the brim with passion and freedom, but I suspected there was a treasure trove of difficulties waiting to be discovered. The sole purpose of my job at Utopia was to help me understand the challenges of therapeutic massage without having to learn how to run a business at the same time. A very practical and sensible plan to launch my free-spirited career, if I did say so myself.

"I'll be right there," I said to Chris as I gripped the phone between my ear and my shoulder, grabbed my purse, and raced out the door.

"Honey," he cooed, in a voice almost as sweet. "There's no reason to be here. They're gone. Poof. Thin air." He lowered his voice to a dramatic whisper. "Why would anyone get involved with the mob anyway? It never turns out well."

I rolled my eyes and shook my head. "Yeah. Well. I

want to see for myself." And I wanted to take a picture to prove to Nash I wasn't making the story up. Not that I was the type to randomly quit a job. And not like Nash was the type to accuse me of lying about my place of employment being randomly closed in the middle of the night. But, you know, just in case.

I scurried out of the coffee shop, taking time to wave at the barista behind the counter, and then hauled myself into my Jeep. The top and doors were off, because duh. Who wouldn't want to soak up all the fresh air and sunshine Galveston, Texas had to offer?

The sun beat down on my neck and shoulders and the heat stole my breath. But once I got moving, the wind blew away the confusion of finding myself suddenly jobless. By the time I arrived in front of Utopia, I was almost giddy at the thought of starting over.

Maybe this was the push I needed.

Maybe Nash was right.

Maybe I had been stalling.

Maybe the universe noticed and decided to shove me out of the nest.

Time to fly, baby girl. Spread those wings and stop coasting.

I smiled and raked a few loose tendrils of red hair back into my ponytail. *Alright then, universe*, I thought to myself. *I'll see your bet and raise you.*

If the powers that be thought it was time for me to move forward with my life, then I would be a fool to ignore the signs. It was time for change! For self-empowerment! For Catherine Wallace to step out of her own shadow and shine!

Chris sauntered my way as I hopped out of the Jeep. His purple hair swooped and swirled around his head, and his muscles bulged under a yellow tank top. White skinny jeans hugged his solid thighs. But for all the color, and there was *so* much color, his personality was the brightest thing about him.

"See," he said, waving a hand at the empty building. "Poof." He made an exploding motion with his hand and let out a puff of air. "Now what?"

Darla arrived beside him, the total opposite of our Magic Man. Where he was color and flash, she was nothing but black upon black upon black. Long, straight, black hair shone down her back. Black eyeliner rimmed her eyes. Black shirt. Black pants. Black shoes. "Yeah," she said with a sigh. "Now what?"

Beside them, I felt unnaturally normal in my shorts, T-shirt, and ponytail. "That is a fabulous question."

"Of course it's fabulous." Chris wrapped an arm around Darla. "That's all I do."

I snapped a picture of the empty store front, then aimed my phone at my friends. Darla scowled while

Chris preened. They both smiled at the image when I showed them. We stood around and chatted about the hows, whats, and ifs for a while before climbing into our respective vehicles in a serious state of confusion.

I picked up my purse and knew instantly something was off. The weight was all wrong. I unzipped it and peered inside. There was way too much space in there. I stared at the yawning, empty bag, my heart yammering away, already aware of what my brain had yet to figure out yet.

Holy.

Crap.

My journal! I had no recollection of it after I set it on the seat beside me at the coffee shop. If it wasn't in my purse, it had to still be there.

Sweat broke out at my temples and I dropped my head on the steering wheel. I had to laugh, or I'd cry. Of all the things I could have forgotten in a public place, it had to be the leather-bound notebook which held all my thoughts, never bothering to censor myself. The one place I was one-hundred-percent honest about what I was thinking, even when it wasn't pretty. Or polite. Or remotely socially acceptable.

Years of *me* lived in those pages. And not the gussied-up version that I presented to the world, but my heart-wrenching moments, my celebrations, my judgements and deep thoughts, my heart and soul.

I smeared my hands over my face, remembering the last entry.

Please, oh please, I thought. *don't let anyone have found it.*

And if they found it, please don't let them read it.

And if they read it, please don't let them still be there when I show up!

After waving goodbye to Chris and Darla, I pulled out of the parking lot and hightailed it right into a traffic jam, distracting myself from the journal debacle by daydreaming about a night alone with Nash now that I didn't have to work. His ring sparkled on my finger and I idly spun it round and round with my thumb while I crawled through the thick traffic, wondering if we could use this time to rekindle some of the fire we had lost. Maybe what we needed was more time together. Maybe the sudden loss of my job was a blessing in disguise.

Nash checked off every box on my dad's list. Wealthy. Driven. Polite. Polished enough to let everyone around him know he came from money.

My mom's list? Not so much.

Though considering she was the complete opposite of my father in every conceivable way, that was no surprise. In the same way that when they got divorced shortly after I entered kindergarten, it wasn't much of a surprise to anyone but little old me.

And my list? How many boxes did Nash check off for me?

See, that's the thing about being raised by two people who see the world in completely different ways. Nash managed to check all my boxes while also somehow leaving them all unchecked. I wanted the predictability he offered but often found myself bored in our perfectly normal life. But, since Dad was living in a comfy home with marble countertops and Mom had her RV parked somewhere in Florida the last I heard, I decided a long time ago to pay more attention to the side of me that agreed with my father.

By the time I made it back to the coffee shop, almost two hours had passed since I left. The chances were slim that my journal was still sitting were I left it. I pushed through the doors and bee-lined for my table. Panic strummed through me for a few terrible seconds that each lasted a year until my eyes fell on a strip of worn leather poking out between the wall and soft cushion of the bench seat. A choir of angels sang. Light shone down from heaven above.

"Thank fucking God," I said, dropping an ultra-rare f-bomb and drawing the attention of a couple of soccer moms who widened their eyes, excited to have something to be offended about. I swooped up the journal and hugged it to my chest as I bounded out the door, crossed the parking lot, and climbed back into my Jeep.

It was a blessing that no one found this thing. In addition to whining about my passionless experiences with my fiancé, I had droned on and on about the meaning of life, written absurd poems, and doodled out my daydreams. There wasn't a more intimate primer on all things Cat Wallace than this journal. I ran a hand over the scarred leather cover and flipped through the pages, shaking my head at my carelessness as years' worth of my looping script blurred in front of me.

Until I got to the last page...

Instead of looping script, I saw tight, formal print...

Instead of blue pen, I saw pencil...

I flipped back to the page and my heart fell into my stomach. That wasn't my handwriting. Someone *had* found my journal. Even worse, someone had read it and felt inclined to reply.

CHAPTER FOUR

I shouldn't have read your journal. I know that. When I found it, I thought maybe I could find your name somewhere on the inside, and that maybe, when I gave it to the barista, he would know you and could give it to you when you returned. I thought I could save you from an invasion of privacy.

But your words caught me and before I knew what I was doing, I was the one invading. I should have stopped, but I couldn't. Your thoughts, the way you see the world...I kept telling myself I'd read one more page, only to continue reading and find something even more beautiful. Or heart-breaking. Or a question so powerful I'd sit back in my chair and ponder the answer.

Your words caught me. They pulled me in, captured my imagination.

I should apologize for the invasion of your privacy, but I can't apologize for this. It's like you were left as a gift for me. A reminder that there are still people in this world worth knowing. Your kindness. Your intelligence. Your insight...

I wish I knew who you were. I wish we could sit and talk, and I could pick that marvelous mind of yours before I set about solving your physical problem.

And believe me, I would solve it.

Every woman deserves to have her body worshipped and if your 'Nash'—I'm sorry, but what kind of name is Nash? Wherever his name came from, if he isn't doing that for you, then he's not worthy of the person I found in the pages of this journal.

I promise you, there is more to sex than a 'second-long dick sneeze.'

If you're with the right person, it is worth starting wars over.

Worth empires collapsing.

Though I'm not sure anything is worth knives in the backs of friends and family.

If I could spend one night with you, I would trace my fingers along your body as you quivered beneath me. I would taste you and tease you, gripping your waist while you arched your back and moaned. I would run my hands along your thighs, lower my face, and lick and suck until you screamed my name. You'd forget the world in your ecstasy and then I'd make love to you while you came and came and came.

I would ruin you for other men, but you would have all the words you could possibly need to describe the sensation. There would be no more gray and ash and boredom. There would be heat so vibrant, the world would catch fire. Your body would be my temple and I would be your savior and you would never feel like an obligation again.

Any man who takes without giving is a fool.

And I'm sorry, but your Nash sounds like a fool.

I, however, am not.

Contact me. Please.

themanwhofoundyourjournal@imail.com

CHAPTER FIVE

C<small>AT</small>

Oh, I was quivering alright, though, I didn't think it was the kind of quivering Mr. X had in mind. How dare he? Not only did he read my journal, but he had the audacity to reply and the balls to believe he could solve 'my problem.'

Of all the cocky, self-assured assholes out there, he had to be the cockiest. The asshole-iest. The...the...the *worst!*

Contact me. Please.

I rolled my eyes. Had he actually believed that would work? That I would read his stupid little note and then be dumb enough to reach out, all wide-eyed and innocent, ready to let a stranger put his hands on me so I could 'forget the world in my ecstasy?' *Thanks, but no thanks, Mr. X.* I knew enough about the world to know not to climb into vans with strangers offering candy.

I tossed my tainted journal on the passenger seat, turned the key in the ignition, and made my way home. Nash would be off work in a couple hours, and I intended to greet him in my sexiest lingerie and highest of heels, a glass of wine in each hand.

I didn't care what Mr. X said, Nash did not take without giving and I was going to prove that tonight. Besides. We had reason to celebrate. Thanks to a little kick in the rear from the less-than-professional-and-possibly-mob-connected owners of Utopia, I was finally going to start my own massage business.

Images brought to life by Mr. X's words distracted me as I drove, and my inner thighs clenched deliciously. I tried to fight off the thoughts, but couldn't stop picturing hands on my body. The hands of a faceless stranger, trailing goosebumps along my skin. His lips, tongue, and teeth teasing moans past my throat. For the first time in a long time, I felt passion—warm and molten—bubbling through my veins.

Feeling guilty, I opted to imagine Nash in place of the highly cocky and inappropriate stranger. All that did was cool the fire, which planted a pebble of sadness in my stomach, so I turned on the radio and sang loudly —and badly—to Taylor Swift the rest of the way home.

Oddly enough, Nash's sleek black Lexus sprawled in the driveway when I pulled onto our street.

Nash never missed work.

Even if he was sick as a dog, he would still suit up and make the drive from where we lived in Galveston to his office in Houston. Once, he stayed at work for fourteen hours with a stomach bug so bad anyone else would have taken a trip to the hospital.

Not Nash.

It was one of the reasons my dad loved him so much. You could depend on Nash Addington to do what was right, come hell or high water.

I hopped out of the Jeep, excitement building in my belly. If Nash wasn't home sick, and of course he wouldn't be home sick, then the only other thing he could be doing is planning to surprise me with something. We had put off getting married for over a year now. The time just never seemed right, with how busy Nash was at work. And because three of our four parents wanted our wedding to be big and showy, a true spectacle for the socially inclined—with the oddball out being my mom, of course—we just kept putting it off.

Sometimes, when we were curled up in bed, me with a book and Nash looking studious with his glasses and laptop, I'd daydream about eloping. Nash wasn't a fan of the idea. Or at least he pretended not to be a fan of the idea. Maybe he changed his mind. Maybe it was all for show. Maybe, he'd been planning it all along and today was officially the first day of the rest of our life.

I bounded up the walk and burst through the front door, dashing my keys on the table and dropping my purse...right next to someone else's. I stared at the thing, refusing to think about what it might mean. Murmured conversation and low laughter sounded from deeper in the house and I followed it down the hallway, bending to pick bits and pieces of women's clothing off the floor until I held an entire outfit in my hand, lingerie and all.

I knew what I would find when I opened my bedroom door. How could I not, given what I held in my hands? But, still, I wasn't prepared for what awaited me when I pushed into the room. My Nash, on my bed, kissing another woman's neck. Cupping her breast. Muttering against her skin the way he used to when we first fell in love. Caressing her. Reveling in her. Completely unaware that I stood there, my stomach in my feet, my heart in my hands, his ring on my finger, and my jaw on the floor.

"What. The. Hell."

Nash lurched out of bed at the sound of my voice. He stood there in front of me, naked, his erection wilting as the woman shrieked and clutched my sheets to her throat. As if I hadn't already seen everything she had to offer. And even I had to admit, what she had to offer was spectacular.

"Cat..." Nash cupped his goods and I scoffed. Like it mattered if I saw him naked or not. I'd been seeing him naked every night for the last seven years. He was, in fact, the only man I'd ever seen naked in person. I was so well acquainted with what he was trying to hide that I couldn't stop from laughing.

"Really?" I pointed at his hands. "Is that really necessary?"

He blinked, but didn't let go, holding onto his bits like he was afraid I'd try to yank them off. I considered it, but decided the effort and subsequent mess wouldn't make me feel any better. He blathered on, making one excuse after another about how innocently he and Camille met and how he never meant for this to happen. All while she continued to shriek and squeal like I had a gun pointed at his head instead of the business end of her thousand-dollar shoe.

I wanted to throw it at his head. First one, then the

other, then each article of clothing, one at a time, just the way I found them. But I didn't. There was something empowering about holding onto her clothes. I stomped around the bedroom, spewing obscenities and waving shoes in his face until my anger threatened to turn into tears. No matter what, I wouldn't let him see me cry. The moment I showed weakness, he'd step in for the kill. He had to see me as a volcano, spewing heat and rage, not a hurt little girl, rejected and crying in the corner.

"Cat..." Nash stepped forward, momentarily holding out his hands until he got a good look at my face. He quickly covered his beans and weenie.

"Save it, Nash. There's not one thing you can say that I want to hear. I've seen all I need to see."

And I had. From a pair of spectacular tatas, to my fiancé's wilting erection, from the tenderness he afforded her, to the disdain in his eyes when I walked in.

It was one thing for our relationship to be a little lackluster in the bedroom department. That was inevitable for all relationships, right? It was an entirely different thing for another woman to have an earth-shattering experience in *my* bed. With my "super dependable" fiancé who never took off work. Unless he was having an illicit affair with someone who still had not stopped shrieking.

"Oh, stuff a sock in it," I growled at Camille, still hugging all her clothes to my chest.

As calmly as I could, because even though I had lost everything today I refused to lose my dignity, I wiggled his ring off my finger and set it on the corner of his dresser. Without another word, I turned on my heel, and walked out of my bedroom, straight down the hallway toward the door. I stopped long enough to grab my purse and my keys, and then hopped into my Jeep, dumping the woman's clothes on my passenger seat. A few miles down the road, I started to laugh. A few miles after that, I started to cry.

CHAPTER SIX

Mr. X

Sometimes, the biggest events in our life go by and we never notice until we look back on things later. Hindsight and all that. Today was not one of those days. Every instinct I had demanded I pay attention. A rattle in the pit of my stomach. The hair on my neck standing on end. A whisper-shout in my head. *Hey, asshole! Pay attention! You're living through one of those moments you're always going to remember.* From today forward, life would be different. I didn't know how. I didn't know why. I just knew.

When I dropped into my favorite seat at my second favorite coffee shop in Galveston and landed right on someone's worn leather journal, I should have taken the thing straight up to the barista. Flipping through the pages? Reading the words? That was an invasion of privacy, and privacy deserved respect. Personally, I would never forgive someone who intruded on my innermost thoughts and had no room in my life for hypocrisy.

But I couldn't resist the feel of the book. The weight of it in my hands. The scent of leather and paper. Judging by the wear and tear on the cover, the worn edges of the pages, this journal had seen a lot of time in someone's hands. I ran my thumb along the paper and then peeked inside, hoping to find the name of the owner.

And that was my first mistake. A few words caught my eye, which led to my second mistake. I cracked the book open and started to read...

...and what I found inside was the most beautiful mind and soul I had ever come across.

Deep thoughts soared across the page. Lyrical things. Sometimes sorrowful, but more often than not, filled with joy or wonder. Beneath the scarred leather cover, I found a woman who looked at this world as if each day was a gift to be unwrapped and savored. A woman who gave and gave and gave to some selfish bastard who seemed more than happy to keep right on taking, and then she wondered why she never felt fulfilled.

The more I read, the angrier I got. Whoever this woman was, she deserved to be surrounded by people who recognized her for the miracle she was. And this Nash? He wasn't appreciating her. He wasn't taking care of her.

He was probably cheating on her and she was too honest to recognize the signs. I wished for a way to tell her he was taking advantage. I wanted to protect her. That's what you did when you found something precious, right? You held it close and kept it away from whatever might destroy it.

And so, it was my protective streak that led me to my third mistake. Instead of snapping the damn book closed and handing it over to a barista, I pulled out a pencil and wrote my mystery woman a letter. I scrawled down my thoughts, a confusing blend of admiration, lust, and a desire to protect her from that jerk of a fiancé. From her perspective, I realized I would be the jerk. The man who chose to peek at the most intimate parts of who she was, and then had the audacity to comment.

The desire to know more about her urged me to give her some way to contact me. So I did what any perfectly rational, anonymous stalker would do. I pulled out my phone and hastily created a new email account, which I then jotted down in the journal. I stared at my words, excited at first, but then concern took over.

The more I thought about how she would see this invasion of privacy, the more I felt like a thief. A traitor. All I wanted to do was reach out and connect with this beautiful soul. In so doing, I painted myself as the kind of man she was already wasting her time with. The kind who took without giving in return. The kind who trampled her needs in favor of his own.

And so, I made my fourth mistake. Instead of waiting for her to return so I could look her in the eyes and explain what happened, I shoved the journal in between the wall and the seat—hoping it wouldn't be found by anyone other than my mystery woman—and left.

CHAPTER SEVEN

FROM: JOURNALGIRL
<getoveryourself@imail.com>
    to: Mr.   X
<themanwhofoundyourjournal@imail.com>
    date: July 20, 2018 at 1:17 AM
    subject: Thanks asshole

I'm just going to jump straight to the point here. What kind of creep reads someone's journal? I mean seriously? What were you thinking? No one knows about the stuff I write in that book. No one. Not my fiancé. Not my friends. Not my parents. Those words were private. Some of them were immature and selfish. Some of them were nothing but pure emotion, scrawled down in the heat of the moment so I didn't do something stupid and say them out loud. Some of them were daydreaming nonsense, my idealistic view of the world.

But here's the thing, NONE of them were for you.

I can't say no one knows that stuff about me anymore because you do. An utter stranger. A selfish jerk. A cocky asshole.

And to make it worse, you decide to comment??

You'd trace your fingers along my body?? Oh yeah?? What right do you have to say something like that to someone you don't know? Are you seriously so conceited that you think you'd have me writhing and screaming your name? You say you're not a fool, but hello! I'd say doing what you did would fit right into the foolish category, wouldn't you?

Although, here I am, sending the email you requested. So maybe I shouldn't be so quick to judge...

Maybe you have more figured out than I give you credit for...

You were right, by the way. Nash really IS a fool. A complete and utter jerk-face and he's the reason I'm drunk right now, which is the reason I'm even writing this email in the first place...because liquid courage for the win! And in case you didn't notice, this is a brand-spanking new email address because DUH. What woman in her right mind would email a stranger using her real address?

And in case you didn't read the 'from' line, it says GET OVER YOURSELF.

The last thing I needed today was you. Like, the complete and utter last thing.

You're in my head now and I'm not sure I want you there. And my whole world got turned upside down and I have no idea what I'm going to do, but every time I close my eyes, I see you. And I don't even know what you look like! So, it's just your words that I see and somehow that's worse because what you said meant something to me.

So, thanks for that.

I need to get my thoughts out of my head before they drive me crazy, but I can't even open my journal because you're there, too. The one place I could go and say the stuff no one needed to hear. The one place I was free to vent and get all the noise out of my head— and believe me, I really need to clear the noise after today. Well, now it's totally contaminated because I flip to the first blank page and there YOU are. What right do you have to say those things about me?

You can't see it, but I'm flipping you the bird right now. And I'm pouring myself another drink. So, I hope you're happy. Because I sure as hell am not.

from: Mr.   X
<themanwhofoundyourjournal@imail.com>
    to: JournalGirl <getoveryourself@imail.com>
    date: July 20, 2018 at 1:30 AM
    subject: RE: Thanks asshole

Am I happy? Yes.

Not because you're unhappy. Not because your world is upside down. Not because Nash is a fool—though I stand by my original statement there.

No, I'm happy because you emailed me.

I didn't think you would.

I haven't stopped thinking about you.

I know it was wrong to read your journal. I know it and I own it, but cut a man some slack here. If you'd opened that book and found *you* inside, you'd have read it, too. Anyone would have. You're captivating. Who wouldn't get a taste of you and want more?

I am, after all, only human. A mere mortal. It would take someone far better than me to find the person I discovered between those pages and then just walk away.

My biggest regret is that I didn't take the time to

cherish each and every word the way it was meant to be cherished. I skimmed, flying through the pages because the more I got, the more I wanted, and I devoured your words like a greedy little boy.

If I had it to do over again, I'd savor each and every page.

I'd read and reread it all until I knew all of you.

And when you got back to the coffee shop, I'd still be there, waiting...

...for you.

Cat

I trembled as I read his words, wanting to be mad at him, but the fire had almost burned itself out. He seemed so genuine. So kind. And as maddening as his invasion of privacy was, it was hard to stay mad at someone who looked at the purest version of me and decided he needed more.

But then again, anyone could be whatever they wanted on the internet. Just because he spoke poetry with his fingers didn't mean he wasn't another selfish asshole waiting to take advantage of me. Maybe he was a pervert. Maybe he did this kind of stuff all the time, and when he succeeded in getting some poor woman to reach out to him, he wheedled his way into her life, then managed to abduct her. Rape. Murder. Who knew what else? The world was full of crazy people willing to do awful things to strangers. Hell, the world was full of crazy people willing to do awful things to the people they loved. Case in point? Nash.

What was this stranger doing up at one thirty in the morning on a week day, anyway? I had every excuse to be awake. No job. No fiancé. No way to sleep in my own bed.

This guy? This Mr. X? What were his excuses for being nocturnal? My guess, they were pretty much in line with mine. No job. No commitments. Probably lived in his mother's basement as he waited for his next victim.

But man, he really knew how to say exactly what I needed to hear...

"Earth to Kitty Cat." Chris sat forward and waved a hand in my face. "You in there? Ready for a refill?" He lifted his empty margarita glass and rattled the ice against the sides.

"No thanks. I'm good. Just got a refill." I locked my phone and flopped back into the chair. "I mean, I'm not good. I'm jobless. Houseless. My fiancé is a cheat. I have no idea what to do next."

"Tell me about it." Chris sighed dramatically, as if

losing his job held as much merit as me losing my job, my fiancé, my home, and my privacy. Though, he didn't know about Mr. X and the journal. After everything that happened, I had to keep that one nugget to myself. Besides, how could I explain the fact that I was oddly touched and that, despite my best interest, I had responded to a man who might be a serial killer.

I closed my eyes and covered my face with my hands. "You know what?" I asked, peeking through my fingers.

"What's that, babycakes?" Chris pursed his lips and did everything but bat his eyelashes as he slid off the couch and ambled into the kitchen for a refill.

"I *am* good. Sure, I lost a lot of stuff. And yes, the winds of change are definitely a-blowin.' But the job wasn't that great. The house felt like a museum. And the jerk-face?"

Chris poked his head around the corner. "Good riddance, right?"

"Exactly. Good riddance." I gave a decisive nod, sloshing margarita onto my jeans. "This is my chance for a fresh start. Shed my old skin. Step out of whatever rut I've dug for myself and make things interesting again." I smiled as I spoke, and then frowned when I realized how much I sounded like my mom. Not that there was anything wrong with sounding like Mom. She was happy. Perpetually. But I just wasn't sure she was the parent I wanted to model myself after considering she gave up her home, and, well, *me*, to roam the world in a broken-down RV.

"Have you heard from the asshole yet?" Chris asked. Neither one of us had spoken his name since I arrived at Chris' apartment. My cheating jerk of an ex-fiancé would be forever nameless.

"I think we said everything we needed to say to each other when I went back to talk to him." I grimaced, remembering the scene when I finally stopped crying and turned the Jeep around. Nash was seething, pacing the house in a pair of PJ pants. He pounced on me the minute I walked through the door. Apparently, his affair was my fault. I had been spinning my wheels, going nowhere. I was a boat anchor tied around his waist, dragging him down and that woman was his lifeline. He was embarrassed of me and was sure my father was, too. When people at work asked him what I did for a living, he couldn't bring himself to admit I was a masseuse. Nash Addington was too big a deal to be engaged to someone who shared genes with a woman who lived in an RV.

"So...really though. What are you going to do?" Chris grazed his shoulder against the doorway on his way through and took a few stumbling steps before collapsing back on his zebra-print couch. "I mean, you're welcome to crash here for as long as you want, but I'm a terrible roommate and this couch is a back problem waiting to happen." He smirked at me over his glass, then downed half the drink in one swallow. That was the beauty of being a bodybuilder, I guess. More mass meant more margaritas.

"Well, when you put it like that..." I grinned at my friend and then sighed. It was a good question. What was I going to do? I hadn't told my dad yet, though I doubted he would be ready to open his home to me, even though he had more than enough space. He based his whole parenting ideology on tough love and had made it crystal clear that the moment I moved out, I was out for good. My mom, on the other hand, would be sure to offer me a place to stay, though I didn't know where I'd sleep in that battered RV of hers.

"Here's what you're going to do," Chris said. "You're going to get your happy ass into the kitchen, make yourself another margarita, and then drink until you can't see straight. We'll solve the rest of your problems in the morning."

His statement made me think of Mr. X promising to solve my physical problem, but I quickly buried the thought in a dark corner in the back of my mind. The last thing I needed was another man, taking up my energy, especially when it would be better spent on me.

"In the morning, huh? Just like that, we're going to make everything all better?"

"Oh, Kitty Cat." Chris winked and tossed his head as if he had long, flowing hair instead of a deep purple crewcut. "Never underestimate the power of too much tequila and a shitty night's sleep."

CHAPTER EIGHT

Lucas

The Hutton Hotel—or The Hut, as we called it—started as my childhood home, a sprawling colonial style house on the beach with more rooms than we had family members. The extra space disquieted Mom, a woman with a heart big enough to love the whole world and the brains to know a business opportunity when she saw one. It didn't take long for the extra rooms to become a bed and breakfast, and for the five blonde children, nut-brown from the Florida sun, well-mannered and polite, to become a selling point to repeat customers.

Soon, the waitlist for a room stretched on for

months and Dad, with Mom's quiet urging, bought a few acres next door and built a series of bungalows to accommodate more visitors. We all helped, or at least he let us think we were part of the process as we handed him hammers and nails. The five of us stood around, staring at the plans with our hands on our hips, too young to appreciate the skill with which our father worked. The bungalows were a hit and the next time we expanded, Dad hired contractors to do the work. The buildings got bigger, the staff got larger, and the Hutton kids grew up.

Mom's desire to heal the world led her to look into health and wellness and Dad's desire to build an empire led him to find ways to monetize Mom's dream. We had cooks that prepared nutritious feasts complete with organic and sustainably grown food. We had masseuses and yoga and meditation nooks with expansive views of the ocean. We had parasailing for the adventurous and soft music for those who needed a quiet place to remember how to breathe.

Our family donated to charities. Built libraries. People didn't just love to stay with us, they loved to work for us, too.

For a heartbeat of time, it was magical.

The memories I had of the early years were covered in sunlight and laughter. We had purpose, even in our childhood. Mom taught us to serve others and Dad taught us how, with enough grit, we could turn a handful of raw materials and a dream into reality

Then Dad started to drink and the magic faded, as it tends to do. As children, we didn't understand. We spent nights whispering, trying to discover what we might have done to make him so unhappy. Looking back, I wondered if maybe Dad wasn't cut out to share his life with so many strangers coming in and out of his home. I had come to suspect that his dedication to Mom's dream was his downfall, though no one, not even the man himself, understood it at the time. Had we known, we'd have stopped. Closed the hotel. Found a new way to make our mark. Huttons stood by each other, which made it all the more difficult when we decided to leave.

As the cab pulled up in front of the resort that was once my home, the familiar view woke something warm and sharp in my heart. Leaving Dad was a necessity, but it went against everything we were taught to value. Being home again felt like I was finally doing my duty, while the child inside me begged to climb back in the cab and disappear. Instead, I paid the driver and unfolded myself from the car, smiling at the white wraparound porch. Palm trees shaded the grass. Ferns drooped from dangling containers. The ocean stretched out forever behind it all.

For all the familiarity, I walked up to the front door with bags on my arms and suitcases trundling behind me, like so many tourists over so many years. The Hut wasn't home anymore, and I was just another person who would come and then go.

The front door swung open. "No shit! Look who made it." Wyatt's wide grin was contagious, his light blue eyes standing out like sea glass in his tan face. He stomped out of the house and wrapped me in a hug, thumping me on the back. "It's good to see you."

I did my best to return the hug around my luggage. "You too, brother. You too."

"Everyone's inside already." Wyatt indicated the house with a jerk of his chin as my mother appeared in the doorway.

Her once red hair was now streaked with gray, though still long and thick and gathered in a braid that fell over her shoulder. Her eyes, the same light blue as Wyatt's, lit up when she saw me, though her cheeks were tear-stained and her smile was sad. "Is that my Lucas?" She pushed through the door with wide arms. I dropped my bags and tucked her against my body. She hugged me like it might be the last time she ever had the chance, a habit she picked up after what happened in Afghanistan.

"Hi, Mom. How are you holding up?"

"I've had good days and bad days." She pulled back enough to look me in the face. "More good days than bad, though." My mother, the eternal optimist. "Come on in. Everyone's here and it's been too long since I had all my people in the same place at the same time."

A look crossed her face, and I wondered if she realized what she said. I stopped thinking of Dad as one of my people a long time ago, too. She led me through the door and my heart stood still. Nothing had changed and I didn't know how to feel about that. Some of the magic from the early years shone from the familiar walls, though fear and anxiety still lurked in the corners. I dropped my bags in the front room and followed Mom into the kitchen, Wyatt trailing close behind.

My brothers and sister waited for me in the dining room, seated around our old oak table. Harlow's long hair, so blonde it was almost white, sparkled in the sunlight falling through the window. She tapped her fingers against the table, a tattoo barely visible on her wrist. Eli, his hair darkened with age, fiddled with a glass. Caleb had his hands tucked behind his head and was staring through a window at the water.

No one spoke and I couldn't tell if the silence was comfortable or awkward or for how long they'd been like that. In years past, the room would have bubbled with conversation and good-natured teasing. Harlow would have been drawing, or writing, or playing her guitar while Eli chattered at whoever would listen, with Caleb adding commentary whenever Eli came up for a breath. Finding them this quiet was like walking in on someone else's family.

Wyatt, his personality a carbon copy of Mom's, stepped past me. "Look who I found." He gestured my way as if presenting a unicorn.

My siblings dropped the quiet act. The sounds of chairs scraping against the wood floor filled the room and they surrounded me with hugs and greetings. Harlow tried to apologize for never coming to see me and I reminded her that I understood.

"Quit cutting her so much slack," Eli said, shaking his head and rolling his eyes. "How's she supposed to learn if you never call her on her bullshit?"

Harlow made a face. "Hello, pot. Meet kettle? Which one of us needs called on their bullshit again?"

"How's the leg?" Caleb asked, stepping forward, arms open. "Still more metal than man?"

I wrapped him in a hug. "For the life of me, I'll never understand why you guys go on like it's a big deal to have shrapnel in your ass."

Wyatt laughed. "Uh. Newsflash. It *is* a big deal to walk around with shrapnel in your ass."

I gave them a rundown of my healing process—

keeping it short and sweet because I didn't need much more than time at this point.

"What are you doing now that you're not a big, bad Marine?" Harlow folded her arms across her chest and gave me a onceover. Her perceptive eyes locked on mine and I knew she saw that I was hiding how lost I felt. Harlow always saw. My sister collected people's stories and catalogued their reactions. A version of this conversation would end up in one of her books and somewhere down the line, I'd have the uncomfortable opportunity to confront myself, the way my sister saw me.

Wyatt dropped a hand on her shoulder then plopped into a chair. "You know what they say. Once a Marine, always a Marine."

I shook my head and filled them in on my life since being released from the hospital, then turned the question around on them. Wyatt had taken over running the resort. Harlow was living in Seattle and still trying to finish her first novel. Eli was working at a bar and had dreams of opening his own—though given our family's history with alcohol, I wasn't sure I understood why. Caleb took tourists out on boats for fishing and exploring. Everyone professed to being happy, but the light I was used to seeing in their eyes had dimmed. It was like looking at a faded photograph. I wondered if they would say the same thing about me.

Was losing the light a natural side effect of growing up? Was the reality of life destined to dull even the brightest soul? Or was this something specific to the Huttons? After all, we'd started out living the dream, only to grow up and meet a monster wearing our father's skin.

We gathered around the table, each of us naturally pulling out the chairs where we sat when we were younger. Slowly, as we talked, things started to feel like they used to. Harlow spun stories so magnificent you couldn't tell where truth ended and fantasy began. Eli poked holes in her logic. Caleb watched thoughtfully.

"You should come with me the next time I take the boat out," Caleb said to her.

Harlow wrinkled her nose. "And smell like worms the rest of the day? No thank you."

Caleb shrugged. "Just sayin'. With fish stories like that, you belong out there more than I do."

"Be careful." She pointed a finger his way. "You keep going on like that and I'll kill you off in my next book. Just ask Luc." My sister had written me into, and killed me off in, more unfinished stories than I could remember.

I leveled her with a glare. "Sure. And maybe this'll be the one you finish."

"Hey!" she cried, sitting up to swat me on my arm. "Maybe I will."

Mom sat and listened, adding exclamations and laughing when we teased each other. I caught her eye and cocked my head, silently asking if she was okay. She took a breath. Her eyes wandered across the faces of her children. She put her hand to her heart and smiled.

CHAPTER NINE

Cat

I woke up hours after I was used to on a typical Tuesday morning, but also hours before I was ready to be awake. Chris wasn't lying when he said he was a terrible roommate. Not only did he keep right on drinking way past my limit, but he also passed out and started snoring on the couch without explaining sleeping arrangements.

Not wanting to commandeer his bed, I tried to sleep tucked into the armchair. Too many margaritas allowed that to work for a while, but I was sober enough after waking up to realize how uncomfortable I was. I snagged a bottle of water out of the otherwise empty fridge and considered making a pot of coffee.

Given the amount of noise coming from Chris' general location, I doubted the hiss and slurp of a coffee pot would wake him, but I didn't want to risk dragging him back to consciousness. I wasn't in the mood for his particular brand of 'handling problems.'

I slunk onto the patio, squinting against the early afternoon sun. At home, I would sit on the deck and watch the ocean when I was stressed—though the sooner I stopped thinking of Nash's place as home, the better off I'd be. Here, I'd have to settle for staring at the burnt grass in the courtyard of the apartment complex while the heat of summer in Texas pushed down on my body.

I stretched in the open air as bits and pieces of my margarita fueled tirade to Mr. X filtered through my memory.

Did I really do that?

Did I really feel compelled to reach out and tell that guy what's what?

I checked my phone and blushed from head to toe. I most definitely did email Mr. X last night and he most definitely responded. At least I had the presence of mind to create a new email account so he couldn't track me down and chop me into bits. I opened the emails and read through them.

If you'd opened that book and found you inside, you'd have read it, too...

I devoured your words like a greedy little boy. If I had it to do over again, I'd savor each and every page. I'd read and reread it all until I knew all of you. And when you got back to the coffee shop, I'd still be there, waiting...for you.

He sure knew how to say all the right things. It was a shame he wasn't a real person.

I had to laugh at that thought. Of course Mr. X was a real person. Obviously, a human made the note in my journal. Also obviously, a human took the time to respond to my email. What I meant was that he wasn't *being* real. He was nothing more than words on a screen. No name. No face. He could be whoever he wanted and after reading my deepest thoughts, of course he knew how to be everything I needed.

The urge to talk to someone beat against my brain. For a split second, I considered replying to his email, but that nonsense needed to stop. Immediately. The last thing I needed to add to my list of tragedies was getting myself kidnapped by a stranger with an email address and the propensity to snoop.

My phone showed zero missed messages or waiting texts from Nash. If the bimbo in my bed wasn't enough to tell me how he felt about me, his utter silence sealed the deal. I pulled up my contacts and almost called my dad, then at the last minute, decided to call Mom. She was breathless when she answered.

"Hey, kiddo! How goes it on this glorious Tuesday? It's Tuesday, right? I swear, time doesn't mean anything anymore."

"Yeah Momma, it's Tuesday. And it goes not so gloriously." I filled her in on all the details, though I left out the bit about the journal. In the scheme of things, that tangent felt inconsequential in comparison to being suddenly single, jobless, and homeless.

Mom sighed. "Oh, Cat." Considering how much she didn't like Nash, the sorrow in her voice took me off guard. "Are we happy or are we sad about this?"

That was a good question. One I didn't know the answer to. I was sad, of course, but I hadn't exactly spent the night in tears. But then again, I wasn't exactly relieved, either. "I'd say we're indignant."

"Indignant is good. Only a fool would behave that way. Cheating is reprehensible."

My mind stuck on the word *fool*, bringing up Mr. X's words and bouncing them around the inside of my skull. "So I've heard," I said. "And yes. It's true. Only a fool."

"What else? Talk to me, Katydid."

I smiled at the nickname, Mom being the only one who ever used it. "I don't know, Mom. I know you didn't like him much..."

"But you did," she said before I could finish, "and that's what really matters."

"Yeah...but..." I took a long breath and then filled her in on the last year with Nash. "And I just kept feeling so bored. I know he was good for me..."

"But was he?" she asked in that way of hers that meant she wanted me to think deeper than I was.

I sighed and then smiled when I realized what she was getting at. "If he was willing to cheat on me, I guess he really wasn't all that good for me, huh?"

Mom made a sound that meant *not really* and then cleared her throat. "And if you're feeling bored and underappreciated..."

I sniffed. "Okay, okay. Maybe he and I really weren't all that great together." I said the words as if they were an epiphany, but it felt more like stating hard truth and settled facts.

I loved Nash. Had since I was seventeen. And I believed he was going to do good things, even if one of those 'good things' was a strange woman with boda-cious boobies. Dad's face, stern yet loving, popped into my brain. *That boy has a good head on his shoulders. The two of you together will make names for yourselves.*

And I had believed him, too. But now, that part of my life was over and I oscillated between grief, anger, and resignation. And despite it all, this little buzz of excitement coursed low and hopeful through my body. I didn't understand the feeling, but I kept finding myself smiling.

"So, what are you going to do?" Mom asked, echoing Chris' question from last night.

"That's the question of the hour, isn't it? The truth is, I'm not really sure. I'm kind of in free fall here. No job. No home. I've got savings, so it won't be hard to find an apartment. It just feels like there's an opportunity here and that I shouldn't act too quickly and squander it."

"An opportunity for what?"

"For change," I said before I even knew I knew the answer.

Mom laughed. "Well, you know how I feel about that 'still-small voice.'"

I shifted in the chair, peeling my sweaty thighs off the plastic, and rolled my eyes. "I know enough to know that you don't go around quoting scripture on the regular."

"It's a great quote, regardless where it came from. I'd be a fool not to use it. Anyway, you have to listen to that stuff. If there's a part of you that's whispering, you have to listen. Life is meant to be lived, not survived. If you're not sure finding an apartment in Galveston is the right answer, then don't do it."

"Says the woman who lives in an RV."

"Yes," Mom said, emphatically. "That's exactly my point. Why settle in one place when there's a whole world to be experienced?"

"Or when you have a child to raise?" I asked the question without bitterness. I made peace with my mom and her nomadic ways a long time ago.

After my parents divorced, Mom won custody and I lived with her until I hit twelve, when she took off on her RV trip round the continent. Dad was more than happy to take me in and erase all the free-thinking she instilled in me and add his dose of sensible cynicism to the mix.

My childhood was split into thirds.

One spent with both of them.

One spent with my mom.

One spent with my dad.

I was a perfect blend of the two most opposite people in all the world.

"Can you imagine how your father would have reacted if I tried to take you with me?"

Honestly, I could. With lots of blustering, furrowed eyebrows, and proclamations that a child needed stability and security. But I let that subject pass, asking instead, "Why did you take off, anyway?"

I had asked the question over and over throughout the years, and the answer she gave me this time was no clearer than any of the rest. "You know how that still-small voice works." She paused and then, "You know you always have a place with me. It's cramped inside, but we have the whole wide world to spread out in. I'm parked in the Keys for a while and there's a resort down here that's hiring. Change of ownership or something. It's been all over the news, though I don't know or care why. Maybe they need a masseuse. Or maybe you don't need a job quite yet and just need to remember what it feels like to live without all that material bullshit keeping you tethered to the ground."

I rolled Mom's statement around. Dad would reject it outright, and if I was being honest, part of me rejected it outright, too. But there was another part calling to me, one that was small and quiet and humming just beneath the surface of my skin. One that told me to stop thinking for a moment and just feel my way to the answer.

I closed my eyes and nodded. "Yeah, Mom. That sounds great. I mean, I can't promise that I'll stay, and I don't even know if my massage license works in Florida, but I'd love to visit you while I figure things out."

She gasped and I heard her fighting tears as we made plans. When we hung up, I took a long pull of my water, steeled myself, and called Dad.

CHAPTER TEN

MR. X

Tuesday became Wednesday and I didn't hear from my mystery woman again. Wednesday became Thursday and I battled myself over whether or not to send her another email. Obsessing over a woman I'd never met with such all-consuming passion fell way outside the range of normal. I knew that. But I worried about whatever it was that had gone wrong in her life and desperately wanted to do something to fix it.

I did everything I could to stop thinking about her, but nothing worked. Her words twined through my head, whispering to me while I worked. A woman whose name I didn't even know was quickly becoming the most important part of my days. It wasn't healthy, but I had the strangest sense that she was worth it. That I was meant to find her journal because…

The thought always stopped right there. I didn't know why I thought I was supposed to find her journal, only that I did. There was nothing logical or sensible about the feeling, but I couldn't ignore it.

I wanted to know what happened and I wanted to help, but more than anything, I wanted to prove to her that I wasn't crazy. And because continually emailing a woman after stealing her most private moments sounded pretty crazy to me, I promised myself I would stay silent unless she reached out again.

That didn't stop me from checking my email obsessively. When nothing new came in, I settled for reading and rereading the one email she sent me, the one that woke me just after my head hit the pillow Monday night.

I assumed the fiancé had done something dastardly, something that made her angry and sad and drove her to drink. Maybe he said something terrible. Maybe he did something terrible. My gut told me she finally figured out he was cheating and my heart broke for her, even though she was better off without him. A soul that pure needed to be loved, not neglected.

Her words kept me company.

You're in my head now and I'm not sure I want you there. And my whole world got turned upside down and

I have no idea what I'm going to do, but every time I close my eyes, I see you. And I don't even know what you look like! So, it's just your words that I see and somehow that's worse because what you said meant something to me.

What she said meant something to me too, but I decided to do the right thing—this time anyway—and keep my distance. The last thing I wanted to be was someone else who took from her without giving in return. So I would do my best to forget her and move on, like any normal man would.

Like she said, I didn't even know what she looked like.

All I had were her words.

And somehow, that was worse.

CHAPTER ELEVEN

FROM: JOURNALGIRL
<getoveryourself@imail.com>
to: Mr. X
<themanwhofoundyourjournal@imail.com>
date: July 26, 2018 at 12:07 pm
subject: hey

I have to hand it to you.

I did not expect you to go radio silent on me.

After nearly a week of not being able to get you out of my head, you win, Mr. X. You win.

You say you got a glimpse into my soul. You say you want more. Well, buckle up cowboy, because here we go.

I think I'm losing my mind. And yes, that's a super

dramatic statement because that's what I put in my journal sometimes—super dramatic statements.

Since you've ruined that for me, you have to deal with my inner monologue of confusion and worry.

Anyway, I'm aware people have gone through so much worse and survived with so much more grace. Maybe my life has been too easy, and things that would seem so small to someone who has truly suffered knock me down hard. Maybe I'm too sensitive. Or maybe I'm just tired of not understanding why I can't find a quiet place to lay my head.

Again, that sounds crazy, especially out of context, but let me explain.

I write my thoughts down in my journal because I've never been able to talk to anyone about the stuff that drives me crazy. For every thought I have, I can see the opposite side of the coin. I can argue it as well as I can argue my original stance because both sides make sense to me.

My friends think I don't know what I want. They think I'm weak. I'm not. I'm just...different.

That's the beauty of being raised by two completely opposite people who are both very smart and both love you very much. I don't have one point of view, molded by two people working together to raise a child. I have two points of view. Sometimes three or four points of view. And I can see the strengths and weaknesses of all the choices in front of me. I try to weigh it all out, but sometimes, the pros balance the cons so well, there isn't a clear winner. Everything looks equally good and bad.

The way I see the world is a constant question mark because I want freedom as much as I want security and I want stability as much as doing the same thing every day bores me.

Can you have security and stability as well as freedom and excitement? It seems like those things are mutually exclusive, one cancels out the other.

Anyway, instead of talking to people, I write to myself. I can get all the thoughts out and argue as many valid points as I can find until I stumble on something that makes sense to me. Does that make me weak? In my opinion, it makes me strong, because I solve every single one of my problems by myself. And that's what I mean about never finding a quiet place to lay my head. When no one fully understands me, it's hard to let down my guard and actually be myself. Around anyone. That sounds way more dramatic than it actually feels. Maybe.

I've never written down my thoughts and worried about someone else reading them before, but the noise in my head is getting too loud for me to handle, and I can't open my journal because you're in there.

I'm starting to wonder if maybe I don't know how

to exist in this world. Or if maybe I'm not made to fall in love with one person and stay that way. How could one person satisfy me when I am *more*? I don't know how to put it other than that. I want everything and that's a horrible thing to admit because I know I can't have it all. And it's selfish of me to expect one person to be everything I need when I've already admitted that the things I need cancel each other out.

I left Nash by the way.

The day you found my journal was also the day I lost my job, which was also the day I came home early and found my fiancé giving all the passionate attention I've been craving...no *needing*...to another woman.

I left with all her clothes. I didn't mean to. They were in my hands and I never thought to put them down and by the time I could bring myself to turn around to give them back, she'd gone home. She probably left in Nash's clothes and my friend says I should laugh at that, and I did, a little, but in the end, I felt bad for making her terrible day worse.

Yes. *Her* terrible day. What if she didn't know about me? What if she thought she was falling in love with the same dependable man I thought I had, only to discover she was the other woman? I would hate myself a little if that happened to me. If I were in her very expensive shoes.

Nash and I fought. It was awful. I had no idea he could be so mean.

Wait. That's not true.

I've seen him be very mean. Nash has no qualms about saying what he needs to say to get what he wants. He'd just never aimed that particular evil power at me before. Anyway, I left him, which means I also lost my home. I'm staying with my mom right now, which is an adventure and has my dad shaking his head, though oddly enough, I think he understands.

And here's the thing. All this chaos in my life should leave me terrified. It should keep me awake at night. It should make me want to curl up and give up, but it hasn't. It's like there's a fire in my belly and it's telling me to grow. To move. To change.

I keep feeling this call to action, but I don't know what that action is. I just know I need to pay attention and listen to everything that's whispering in my ear and you know what? The one thing that's whispering the loudest is YOU.

Your words to me. All 480 of them. That's right, I counted them because I can't stop reading them. And I can't stop reading them because I can't stop wondering who you are and if you mean what you say.

And, just so you know, I'm still furious at you for reading my journal. The easiest way to explain what you did is to say you stole from me, but it's so much worse than that. You didn't steal a *thing,* something I can replace. You stole...me.

But I'm also touched that you saw every ugly thought in my head, every wild daydream, every childish fantasy, and it didn't scare you away. In fact, you looked right at all the things that make me who I am and called me beautiful.

So here I am, Mr. X. I'm an open book. Ask anything you want, and I'll answer.

---

from: Mr.   X
<themanwhofoundyourjournal@imail.com>
     to: JournalGirl <getoveryourself@imail.com>
     date: July 26, 2018 at 12:15 pm
     subject: RE: hey

Are you okay?

---

from: JournalGirl <getoveryourself@imail.com>
     to: Mr.   X
<themanwhofoundyourjournal@imail.com>
     date: July 26, 2018 at 12:16 pm

subject: RE: re: hey

I open myself to you and you go with 'are you okay?' Way to waste an opportunity.

That's a joke, by the way. I cried when I read your question. Thank you for caring.

I'm fine. A little lost, a little confused, a little hopeful. Now please, hit me with something better than that.

---

from: Mr.   X
<themanwhofoundyourjournal@imail.com>
    to: JournalGirl <getoveryourself@imail.com>
    date: July 26, 2018 at 12:25 pm
    subject: there is no better than that

Of course that's the first question I'm going to ask. Your whole life is upside down and you're swimming through rough seas and before I can get into 'something better than that' I need to know you're really okay.

Why are you so ready to pour your heart out to me? You do know it's dangerous to talk to strangers, don't you?

---

from: JournalGirl <getoveryourself@imail.com>
    to: Mr.   X
<themanwhofoundyourjournal@imail.com>
    date: July 26, 2018 at 12:26 pm
    subject: looking stern

Are you telling me not to talk to you?

---

from: Mr.   X
<themanwhofoundyourjournal@imail.com>
    to: JournalGirl <getoveryourself@imail.com>
    date: July 26, 2018 at 12:27 pm
    subject: look stern all you want

No. Definitely talk to me.

Why lost? Why confused? When there's hope, cling to that. Life is crazy and change is inevitable. Sometimes it's violent. Sometimes it's beautiful. Sometimes it's both. The best any of us can do is know what we need and learn how to be happy along the way. To find a handful of people who cherish us and hold them close, because this journey is a doozy.

The things that matter most aren't actually things.

They're the odd moments of understanding.

The breath in our lungs.

The blood in our veins.

The smile on the face of someone you love, of someone who loves you in return.

CHAPTER TWELVE

C<small>AT</small>

Sweat trailed down my back as I finished reading X's email, parked in the sweltering heat of the Florida Keys. In front of me sprawled what had once been a stately home, but was now a luxury resort. As I took in the details, I came to the conclusion that whoever decided to name this place The Hutton Hotel lacked imagination. Nothing about the name evoked the pristine landscaping and sprawling buildings nestled against the ocean, oozing southern charm. The website boasted almost fifty rooms, yet the site was serene and calm and the furthest thing from the typical tourist traps found all too frequently along the beaches in the Keys.

The email needed a response, but I couldn't wrap my head around what to say yet. His words touched me. They made sense in a way not many people ever did. If he was standing next to me, I would put a hand on his arm. I would smile at him. I would take a breath and shake my head and let him see exactly how deeply he touched me.

But he wasn't here. He was somewhere back in Galveston, maybe sitting at the coffee shop, watching to see if he could figure out if I was there, too. I wondered, if I was still in Texas, would I go back to that coffee shop? If I was really honest with myself, I wanted to. I wanted to see this man who managed to make me hopeful while my life crashed down around me, who made me feel beautiful when the rest of the world considered me a bit of an odd duck.

I decided to let my response marinade in my subconscious for a bit, locked my phone, and dropped it into my purse before hopping down from the Jeep. The air seethed with humidity. I smoothed my hair and adjusted my skirt before crossing the lot and climbing the steps to an elegant wraparound porch. Ferns hung in pots and swung in the breeze that cooled the sweat at my temples.

The hotel looked more like a home than a place of business and I hesitated, unsure if I should knock or step inside. A sign on the door read Please Come In, so with one last deep breath, I did just that.

The décor on the inside matched the outside—easy, pristine, welcoming. A hand drawn chalk sign pointed me toward the office and I stepped through a wide doorway into a room dominated by oak bookshelves, windows with streaming sunlight, and a heavy oak desk. Potted plants and orchids added color to the richly decorated room, but they were not what had my attention.

A man sat at the desk, his head bowed as he studied papers spread out before him, every bit as imposing as the furniture. Large hands ran through thick, honey-blonde hair. A white button down shone against tan skin, the top two buttons undone. I couldn't look away. I couldn't move. The sight of him froze me in place while my nerves sang with…what?

What was I feeling, looking at this man? Something I had never felt before, of that I was sure.

He smiled to himself before glancing up to look at me. The smile faded when our eyes locked.

He took my breath away as he shifted in his seat, his movements slow and confident. His eyes traveled across my face and body and I sucked in my lips as I smoothed my skirt, suddenly feeling underdressed.

This man exuded confidence and control. He was a warrior. A Viking. Standing before him, I felt small and helpless. Time stopped as he studied me, then his gaze fell on something over my shoulder and the spell was broken.

"You must be Catherine." The voice came from behind me and I turned to find another man, less imposing than the first. Good humor twinkled in his eyes. "I'm Wyatt Hutton. That there is my older brother Lucas." He indicated the man behind the desk with a jerk of his chin as he offered me his hand.

"Please," I said, swallowing hard as I glanced back at Lucas. "Call me Cat."

Wyatt nodded. "Cat it is. Normally I do my interviews in the office, but Lucas is busy doing..." He leaned through the doorway and stared at his brother. "Just what are you doing in there again?"

Lucas leaned back and folded his hands behind his head. "Pretty sure I'm doing your job, aren't I?" He cocked an eyebrow at Wyatt who laughed, while I trembled at the sound of his voice.

"Only because I couldn't trust you with Cat, here." Wyatt turned his attention back to me. "You and I can talk in the other room so the big bad wolf can finish pretending to do my job."

Lucas rolled his eyes and gave me his full attention once again. My stomach fluttered and my thighs clenched, sending a rush of blood to warm my cheeks.

I had often wondered what it would be like to have

someone see all of me. In a way, Mr. X had when he read my journal, but I hadn't been there when it happened. The reality of Lucas' sharp eyes dissecting my every move was off-putting. I glanced away to buy myself a chance to breathe, then brought my gaze back to his so as not to be rude.

"It's a pleasure to meet you," he said in a voice like smoke and wood and leather. And with that, he gave his attention back to his work and I drew another ragged breath.

Wyatt led me into what looked like a sitting room. He lowered himself into a plush leather chair, indicating one for me. Acoustic guitar music filtered through an open door in the back.

"That's my sister." Wyatt glanced toward the door. "If it bothers you, I'll holler at her."

"It's lovely," I said. "No need to ask her to stop."

The look on Wyatt's face made me think I passed some kind of test, though I couldn't imagine what that test could be. The family resemblance between the brothers was strong and I wondered if the sister shared the same incredible genes. Was she as beautiful as her music? As imposing as Lucas? As genuine as Wyatt?

Wyatt picked up a paper from the coffee table. I recognized the resume I cobbled together using Chris' laptop before I left Galveston. He studied it, his brow furrowed. "No home address?"

"I'm new to the area." I explained the Nash situation, being honest without going into too much detail. "I'm staying with my Mom until I find an apartment and she doesn't exactly have an address."

My answer confused him, as it should. I painted a verbal picture of my mother's free spirit, the RV she called home, and my desire to know I was gainfully employed before I signed a lease anywhere else. Wyatt listened carefully and without judgement. He asked questions about my previous employment, about my training and licensing, and about my plans for the future. The interview felt like a conversation between friends and Wyatt seemed pleased with my answers.

"Wyatt?" Lucas stepped into the room. His gaze fell on mine and my body went on high alert, butterflies in stomach, heart pounding, chest heaving. I purposefully looked away to break the spell, but it didn't work. His mere presence interrupted the flow of blood to my brain. "Mom needs you in the office," Lucas continued, oblivious to my reaction. "Think I can finish this up for you?"

"All that's left is the tour." Wyatt stood. "I suppose even you could handle that." He paused next to Lucas on his way out of the room and engaged him in quiet conversation, presumably about me. When they finished, Wyatt lifted a hand in my direction, apologized for the interruption, and disappeared from view.

While I melted into a puddle of intimidation and lust, Lucas explained the set-up of the hotel. Some of the guestrooms were here in the house, but the majority of the guests stayed in bungalows that stretched along the beach. "My brothers and I helped build the first bungalows, though as The Hut grew in popularity, Dad hired a contractor to construct the rest."

As he explained the history of the hotel, I fell in love with the idea of a family working and growing together. I wondered about the rest of the Huttons, but Lucas guided the conversation to other things and the time to ask was gone. He spoke with soft confidence and I wondered about the warrior I thought I saw when I first walked into the office.

Our gazes kept locking and my body kept rioting. I had to keep reminding myself that this was more than a conversation with an interesting stranger. This was a job interview and I'd be smart to remember that.

Outside of running my own wellness spa, I couldn't ask for a more perfect job. The Hutton Hotel boasted open air massage stations overlooking the water. Top end essential oils. Training in the latest and greatest techniques if I was so inclined.

"And," Lucas said. "It's not uncommon for some our employees to stay in the resort while they get settled in the area. We deduct costs from your paycheck and offer an impressive discount. When you work for the Huttons, you're part of the family. If you need a place to stay, you have one." He explained the details and costs and my eyes widened in shock.

While staying with Mom cost significantly less than staying here, sleeping on a foldout bed that doubled as a kitchen table appealed to me about as much as going back to Galveston and begging Nash to let me move back in with him. "Those numbers are hard to resist."

"You haven't even seen the rooms yet." He smiled and it was like the sun breaking through the clouds and dancing across the waves. Warmth brightened his face and settled comfortably in my soul. "Come on, let me show you where you'd stay."

Lucas offered me his hand. I took it, his skin rough and worn against mine. This man knew hard work. For as comfortable as he looked behind the desk, I wondered how much time he actually spent there. I imagined him with a hammer in his hand, or a shovel, or a saw, his body glistening in the sun while he worked.

The image sent a surge of adrenaline into my belly, reminding me to stop imagining him as anything but my boss. Or my boss' brother. Either way—the fact that he continued to be naked in my imagination had to cross a line...somewhere. The only man I was allowed to react to at all was Mr. X and that was only because he was more like a journal that talked back than an actual human being. Nameless. Faceless. Bodiless.

Safe.

Lucas led me upstairs to show me the rooms they offered to employees in need. They were small and on the third floor of the main house, but sunlight filtered through windows with exquisite views of the beach. Simple yet lavish furnishings made the small spaces seem luxurious. The rooms had balconies. They were also small, but there was enough room to sit outside and drink coffee, and, if I was careful, to do my morning yoga.

"We don't have many rooms open up here." Lucas pointed to a closed door. "I'm in that one right now. My sister's in there. And the two brothers you haven't met are there." He pointed to three doors in turn. "If you decide to stay at The Hut, that one would probably be yours," he said, pointing to the door next to his. The thought of falling asleep with little more than drywall and two-by-fours separating me from Lucas was enough to make me smile. He glowered at me and walked away, leaving me to trail after him like a lost puppy.

While Lucas led me around the rest of the complex —pointing out the bar, the kitchens, the yoga studio, the meditation room—that still-small voice inside me whispered. *Do it, Cat. Do it.*

When he showed me the massage area, that voice stopped being small. This was it. Whatever it was that I had been holding out for, it was right here. Lucas watched my reaction, his gaze laser-focused and direct. I felt the weight of it as I wandered the well-appointed room, daydreaming about all the good I could do in a space like this.

When I turned to him and caught his eyes, that still-small voice gasped. *This!* it yelled, though I didn't understand what it meant.

"Have I sold you, yet?" he asked.

"Does that mean I have the job? Because I was sold before I walked through the front door."

"That's funny. You were hired the minute your resume hit Wyatt's desk. The interview was just a chance to make sure you weren't a serial killer hiding behind a stellar background."

"And an hour was all you needed to know that I'm not a killer?"

Lucas laughed, a low sound, warm and sensuous. "I'm an excellent judge of character."

I stammered out a reply, something that would surely embarrass me if I could think straight enough to know what I said. As things stood, I was pleased to have managed to say anything at all.

He guided me back to the main house where we set up a date for me to come back and fill out my new-hire paperwork. He walked me to the front door and then paused. "It was truly a pleasure meeting you, Cat." His eyes traveled across my face and held me in place.

I dropped my gaze to give myself a moment to breathe and then smiled up at him. "You too, Lucas. I'm very excited."

"You should be." He placed a hand on my arm. "We're very excited to have someone like you join our family."

His touch was fleeting and gentle, but it felt like the onset of a storm. A flash of lightning with the long rumble of thunder rolling behind, the beginning of something violent and beautiful.

We said our goodbyes and I climbed into my Jeep just as my phone pinged. Excitement danced in my belly as it always did now that Mr. X and I were emailing. The excitement sputtered out when I found a text from Chris, informing me I was a hooker for finding a job as glorious as this one. Apparently, he had done a little research on The Hutton Hotel and came to the same conclusion I had: this was one hell of a place to work. I shot off a reply.

I just finished the interview. How would you know if I had the job? Maybe I bombed.

Chris responded a second later.

This is you we're talking about. Of course you got the job. Bitch.

I shook my head and then opened Mr. X's last email to me, sighing as I read it again. The man had poetry in his soul, that was for sure.

My smile came easily as I drove back to where Mom's RV was parked, daydreaming about my future here in the Keys, deciding what I was going to say in my next email to Mr. X, while remembering the rough feel of Lucas' hand against my own.

CHAPTER THIRTEEN

Lucas

"Well?" Wyatt asked as I stepped into the office. "What did you think?"

For a moment, he looked like our father, standing near the windows, backlit by the sun. I blinked and the moment was gone. Running a hand along the back of my neck, I squinted at him as I worked on a sore spot in my shoulder. "Of the masseuse?"

"No. Of the broccoli." Wyatt laughed and sat behind the desk. "Yes, of course of the masseuse."

"She seems great."

And by great, I meant amazing. Beautiful. Witty. Driven. Kind. Intelligent. Her laugh was pixie dust. The smile on her face etched itself into my brain. The wind had blown her hair into her eyes and she'd brushed it away. I had stood there, staring, wondering what it would be like to touch her. Was her skin as soft as it looked? Were her breasts as perfect as I imagined? What would she look like, sprawled underneath me, pleasure contorting her face? I couldn't look at Cat without resenting every stitch of clothing covering her from view. Her body lit mine on fire and it was all I could do to maintain an air of professionalism around her.

"Great?" Wyatt leaned his elbows on his desk. "We get an applicant like that once in a blue moon and all you can say is that she seemed great. You've been gone too long, brother. If you knew the kinds of people I've had to turn down…" My brother rolled his eyes and shuffled papers, a crease appearing between his brows. He pinched his forehead with his thumb and forefinger and sighed. Stress clung to him, tension tightening his normally open features. Maybe that was why he looked so much like Dad moments ago.

I took a stab at what bothered him. "Were you and Mom able to work through that accounting error? Is it as bad as it seemed?" Dad had been in charge of the money before he passed. Either his brain was more pickled than we ever knew, or he had gotten into some shady shit because Burke Hutton had been too smart to have discrepancies like the one I found floating around.

Wyatt let out a long breath. "It's bad. It won't kill us, but we need to go through everything with a fine-toothed comb. If we find more errors like that..." He stared at his feet and I could almost read his mind, a series of ever-worsening curses flung toward our father. Even in his death, he managed to hurt us.

"So, I was right about Cat, wasn't I?" Wyatt asked after a few minutes. "She's exactly the kind of person we want working here." He peeked at me, a smile quirking his lips, and the ghost of our father left his face. "Please tell me you didn't do that thing you do."

"That thing I do?"

Wyatt folded his arms behind his head and smirked. "Yeah. You know. That thing where you get all intense and glowery and intimidate the hell out of people?"

"Glowery?" I asked. "What the hell are you talking about?"

"I assumed they beat it into when you joined the Marines. Even I have the urge to scream 'Sir, yes Sir!' at you from time to time." He lifted a hand in mock salute and squared his shoulders before laughing lightly and resting his elbows on the desk.

"We made an appointment for her to come in next week and fill out all the paperwork." I smiled, knowing he'd be thrilled by my news.

Wyatt stood, bobbing his head. "That's fantastic.

Just based on her experience, she'd be a solid hire, but I can't shake this feeling that she could be so much more for the hotel than just a masseuse. You know Mom's always looking to put more focus on the health and wellness side of things. Maybe Cat's the piece that's been missing."

"Maybe she is."

His words hung in the air between us.

Maybe Cat's the piece that's been missing.

He was right. I didn't know how, but he was right.

Wyatt stared out the window for a few seconds before turning back to me. "You offered her a room, right? Sounds like she's living through a rough patch."

I wondered about the rough patch but didn't ask, even though I wanted to. Her problems were none of my business. At least that's what I kept telling myself as I battled the strongest urge to protect her from whatever she was dealing with.

Pushing away the strange thoughts, I refocused on Wyatt. "She tried to turn us down, but once she saw the numbers she changed her mind."

"Mom will be pleased."

Right around the time The Hut moved out of the bed and breakfast arena and grew into a full-blown resort, Mom suggested opening the rooms in the house for employees in need. Dad cursed her for years over it, but she stood her ground. He swore up and down that they were losing money hand over foot because of her generosity. And maybe they were, but her argument held weight, they had money to spare.

"She should be," I said to Wyatt and then crossed the room to lean over the desk. While he filled me in on the mess Dad left behind, my thoughts wandered back to Cat, replaying each and every moment we spent together. Monday couldn't come quickly enough. I wanted to know more about her. Hell, I wanted to know *everything* about her. I didn't think I had ever met a woman so beautiful. So poised. So...

"Hey." Wyatt leaned forward to catch my attention. "You in there?"

"Yeah. Sorry. I got lost in thought."

"You think?" Wyatt pushed off the desk and stared out the window. "How long do you think it'll be like this?"

"Like what?"

"All of us here. Working together."

I stared at his back as I tried to find the answer. How long could I stay here? With Dad gone, it was easier to breathe, that was for sure. But he was still everywhere. In the accounting. In the buildings. In the stories I had to tell Cat. He was built into the history of this place. Being with my family felt good, especially after everything I went through last year, but how long could that last? It had been years since we all lived together and each of us had been busy building our own lives.

"How am I supposed to know that?" I finally answered.

"I don't know." Wyatt shook his head and crossed his arms, dipping his chin. "It's good having you back. All of you." He turned. "Mom hasn't smiled this much in a long time."

I knew Mom wanted her children to come home. She wanted us to take over parts of the hotel. She wanted us to run The Hut as a family. It sounded good...and bad. Could my brothers and I drop our lives to come home? Could Harlow stop wandering? There could be healing here, but there could also be destruction.

"I don't know, man," I said to Wyatt. "We'll take it one day at a time, I guess."

He blew a long breath through his nose, stared me in the eye, and then swiped the papers off the desk and continued explaining what he found.

CHAPTER FOURTEEN

CAT

I spent the weekend getting to know my mom again. We'd stayed in touch over the years, talking to each other at least once a week, but living with someone makes it impossible to smooth over the prickly bits the way you could over the phone. She had changed. A lot.

Age sat heavily on her shoulders. She moved slower. She groaned when she changed positions. She sighed deeply at times, and didn't seem to know she was doing it. Gray tinged her hair, her skin, her spirit. But her face lit up every time she looked at me and I regretted not visiting sooner.

As I pulled up in front of her RV after my second meeting at The Hutton Hotel, she sat in a white plastic lawn chair, staring at the sky, her face slack. The moment she heard my engine, she pivoted, pressing her hands into the chair to stand. The most beautiful thing about my mother had always been her smile—a trait I hoped I'd inherited—and she flashed it at me as I killed the engine.

"There's my Katydid," she said as I turned off the Jeep and hopped down. "Get everything squared away? Are you officially an employee of The Hutton Hotel?"

I nodded and ran a hand over my hair to tame the flyaways caused by the wind. "Who knew it took so much paperwork just to start working for someone? I think I'm responsible for the death of a small forest."

Mom studied my face for a long moment. "Was your seething warrior there?" A glimmer of her younger self twinkled in her eyes.

"Mom!" I grabbed our second plastic chair—this one much newer, purchased just for me—from its place near the RV and set it next to hers. "My seething warrior? Really?"

"Oh, come on. Let an old woman live vicariously through her beautiful daughter. Did he pull you close? Were deep, meaningful looks exchanged? Was there, perhaps, dare I say it, bodice ripping?"

I rolled my eyes and settled back into the chair,

drawing in a deep breath of fresh air. "You spend too much time alone, you know that?"

"I do." Mom smiled sadly and then waved her hand. "But my life was my choice so I'm not complaining. Now. Details." She looked at me expectantly and I laughed.

Mom had never mentioned being lonely before. I always assumed she was happy with her life. "Actually," I said, "his almost-as-cute younger brother was there instead."

"Bummer...?" Mom's face was a question mark.

"You are something else, you know that? I was a tiny bit disappointed when Lucas wasn't there, but Wyatt is very easy to be around. I like the Huttons, or, at least the two I've met."

Mom tried on their names, rolling them around in her mouth like she was tasting wine. I watched her, trying to put a finger on all the ways her face had changed in the last year. "What?" she asked. "Lucas and Wyatt Hutton. Very strong. Traditional. Keep talking." She grinned and I saw my mom again.

"Anyway," I said on a sigh. "It's probably for the best that Lucas wasn't there, you know? It's too soon after Nash and I'm not gonna lie, the physical chemistry is off the charts between us. He intimidates the hell out of me, which I thought would be a turn off." I gave my mom a tentative look. "It's not," I admitted. "Not at all."

But, since my physical side seemed to be broken right now—what with the absent orgasms and all—pursuing anyone for that reason was a foolish endeavor. I couldn't tell Mom that, though. Nor could I tell her about the poetic stranger I'd been emailing. Of all the people in my life, my mom would understand, but I just wasn't ready to talk about Mr. X yet. Talking about him would make him real, and I'd have to accept that while I was slowly falling for a man I had never met, I was intensely attracted to my boss' brother.

Every time I thought of Lucas, my stranger's words hummed through my mind. The physical and the mental, twining together. For some reason, pursuing Lucas felt like an affront to Mr. X, even though we hadn't exchanged names.

"You're being too cautious." Mom eyed me as if she could see right into my head and knew exactly what I was thinking. Knowing Mom, she probably could. She read me better than anyone. "There's no harm in looking, Katydid. Not much harm in touching either."

"Mom!" I pushed out of my chair while she cackled merrily, pleased to have shocked me.

"The whole world is caught up in timing, as if there's a perfect time for everything to happen. Like we can schedule ourselves right down to the minute. It's not natural. If the right person appears in your life, does it really matter when?"

What if there's more than one? What if the right person is actually the right people? What then?

The thought hit me so hard it almost jumped out of my mouth, but I caught it and swallowed it down. "You want something to drink?"

Mom shook her head and started a discussion about dinner. All weekend, moments like this had kept me from telling her I'd decided to stay at The Hut. As much as I didn't like sleeping on the fold out, I loved spending time with Mom. Over the years, I had forgotten how easy it was to drop all the pretense and just *be* with her. But, if I waited any longer to tell her, it would be cruel.

"Hey, listen," I said and then trailed off as the smile brightening Mom's face slowly disintegrated.

"I'm not going to like this, am I?"

"How do you do that?"

"Do what?"

"Take one look at me and know exactly what I'm going to say?"

"For one thing," Mom said. "I don't know exactly what you're going to say, only that I won't like it. And for another? You have the worst poker face I've ever seen. You wear your heart on your sleeve. It's one of the things I love the most about you."

I steeled myself and delivered the news. "It's a great deal and there's a real bed."

"It is hard to pass up on a real bed," Mom conceded.

And with that, the conversation moved on.

CHAPTER FIFTEEN

FROM: JOURNALGIRL
<getoveryourself@imail.com>
    to: Mr.   X
<themanwhofoundyourjournal@imail.com>
    date: August 1, 2018 at 11:38 am
    subject: Holy WOW, Batman!

I spent the last couple days trying to figure out how to respond to you. I wanted to come at you tit for tat. You hit me with some deep truths. I wanted to have some deep truths to throw right back your way.

After days of thought, all I have for you is WOW!

Yes.

You nailed it.

When you boil life down to its essence, what matters most is who and how you love.

I wonder, what have you lived through to find such wisdom? Deep heartache? Loss? Are you a young man or an old man? I'd expect you to be older with truth like that living inside you, but, all the cocky BS you left in my journal makes me think you're younger.

Is that too much to the point?

Am I being too direct?

Under normal circumstances, I think the answer would be yes. But, considering what you said to me in my journal, it seems like you don't care too much for formality and manners.

So, I ask, how old are you, Mr. X? What have you lived through that brought so much wisdom your way?

---

from: Mr.   X <themanwhofoundyourjournal@imail.com>
    to: JournalGirl <getoveryourself@imail.com>
    date: August 1, 2018 at 11:55 am
    subject: HEY THERE!

I can't tell you how glad I was to see your name in my inbox. =)

I guess you're right. I really did blast past all the formalities of politeness and manners, didn't I?

I'm 31. Does that make me an old man or a young man?

Your question made me realize how much I don't know about you. Your name. Your age. What you do for a living. And yet, I feel like maybe I know you better than anyone else in your life. I couldn't pick you out in a crowd. I don't know your favorite color. Or your favorite kind of music.

But I know the sunrise makes you smile. I know you sit outside as often as you can because the vastness of the sky, the birds calling to each other, the hum of cars in the distance, the vague hints of conversation, they all make you feel connected, like you're part of something bigger than yourself.

I know you cry easily, and you hate it.

I know you are loyal to a fault.

I know you can find beauty in a blade of grass.

And I know you hate raisins as much as you hate feeling taken for granted.

Maybe those minor details like your name, your age, the color of your hair, maybe they don't matter, because I know *you*. I couldn't care less about the packaging around oatmeal cookies. They could come wrapped in a plain paper bag and they'd still be my favorite.

As for me and my 'wisdom' as you call it, my mom would say I came this way. I value introspection and growth. I've always seen the world differently than anyone else, though I think we all say that, don't we? To some degree, we all feel like islands, surrounded by people facing slightly different directions, heading down slightly different paths. I wonder how many people actually find someone who meets all their needs, agrees with all their beliefs...

We are each so unique, finding a perfect match might be a fool's errand.

But there I go again, wandering off after a thought, too shiny not to follow.

You're right, by the way. I lived through some stuff that spurred my introspection on to a whole new level.

Will you tell me your name?

---

from: JournalGirl <getoveryourself@imail.com>

to: Mr.   X
<themanwhofoundyourjournal@imail.com>

date: August 1, 2018 at 11:58 am

subject: nope.

Really? You read my whole journal. You know the best

and worst of me in a way no one else does and you're going to avoid my question with an answer like 'I lived through some stuff?' Hardly seems fair, now does it? If you can't tell, I'm unimpressed with your answer.

---

from: Mr.   X
<themanwhofoundyourjournal@imail.com>
    to: JournalGirl <getoveryourself@imail.com>
    date: August 1, 2018 at 12:15 pm
    subject: RE: nope.

When you put it like that, no it doesn't seem fair at all.

Do you know how many times I've started typing away, trying to explain what happened to me, only to erase it all and start again? This is probably my fourth start on this paragraph. It's hard, baring myself to you like this. I can see now why you consider me a thief. There's nothing more personal than the deepest parts of who we are, and I took those from you without asking. Again, I apologize. But at the same time, I'm not sorry at all. It was wrong of me to take what wasn't given, but if given the chance, I would gladly make the same choice. Think of me what you will.

As far as the stuff I lived through...

I died last year. I came back, obviously. And I wasn't dead long. But there were times, especially at first, that I wished I'd stayed wherever it was I went.

Coming back was hard. It changed everything. I realized how fragile we all are. I realized that so much of what we cherish means nothing in the end. I was alone through a lot of my recovery and I kept wondering why I was fighting so hard. Why battle through it all when I had nothing to battle for...?

I'm sure I'm making a mess of this description, but the biggest thoughts are the hardest to articulate. It's probably why so many of us settle for less than our best. Chasing down new ideas means we have to stretch and sometimes that's uncomfortable.

Honestly, there's no 'sometimes' about it. Change sucks and it's easier to settle for the devil we know than to risk opening our life to the possibility of even more hellfire and brimstone.

Anyway, after my family showed up, my recovery got easier. I stopped fighting life and started fighting *for* life. The whole experience brought everything into focus and now, well, now I know that I would do anything for the people who love me. And it leaves me feeling a little lost because so much in our lives is built around *stuff* and *things*. We champion the selfish...

"Be true to yourself! Go your own way! Find your

passion! Be real! Buy our stuff and you'll be happy/you'll show them/you'll know you've arrived!'"

Arrived? The only place we're aiming for is the grave. Life is movement, sometimes fluid and graceful, sometimes harsh and jolting, but things are always moving and changing. I don't want to 'arrive' because that means it's time to stop. I fought too hard to ever stop again.

Life is supposed to be about the journey, but all too often, we're so focused on where we think we're going, we never appreciate where we are. I can't tell you how many times I thought I would finally be happy when I achieved this goal, or obtained that thing, only to get there and find myself still craving more. So I'd change the goal. Or find a new thing. It's a constantly moving goalpost of unfulfillment.

It's all so hollow, but it's the only way people relate to each other—name brands and life goals and the like. And now that all I want to do is slow down and simplify and draw my family close, it's like I'm standing alone while everyone wonders what the hell I'm going on about. Last year, I opened my eyes and saw everything there was to see and it's AMAZING, but everyone else is standing next to me with their eyes squeezed shut, trying to get me to understand why I sound crazy. I just want to shake them. To yell at them. OPEN YOUR EYES...!

When you boil it all right down to its essence, that's why I left you that note in your journal. It's why I stole your thoughts, your dreams, your fears, and your passions. Because I saw something beautiful and I couldn't let the moment pass without speaking up. Life is too short and too fragile not to say what you mean and go after what you want. Why sit frozen in fear when you can *move*?

Speaking of your journal, I have to ask, have you found a solution to your problem yet?

And please, what's your name?

---

from: JournalGirl <getoveryourself@imail.com>
    to: Mr.   X
<themanwhofoundyourjournal@imail.com>
    date: August 1, 2018 at 12:30 pm
    subject: you don't give up, do you?

Found a solution to my problem? I suppose you mean the problem that brought us together in the first place? The problem that spurred the most embarrassing journal entry of all time?

No. I have not. But, given all the stress of discovering a cheating fiancé, I suppose that's natural. It's not like I've had a chance to really experiment all that much either.

And for the record, no, I'm not comfortable talking about this.

I'd rather talk about you.

You died??

And you're back??

I have so many questions and I'm not sure they're mine to ask. All I can say is that I'm glad you're back. And I'm glad you didn't censor yourself when you found my journal. I might have been furious with you at first, but now, I guess I feel touched to have mattered. And I'm glad that we're talking. Glad to get to know you. The world needs more people like you.

It's funny that you keep asking for my name without bothering to sign your own. I'll show you mine if you show me yours?

Katydid

---

from: Mr.   X
<themanwhofoundyourjournal@imail.com>
    to: JournalGirl <getoveryourself@imail.com>
    date: August 1, 2018 at 12:32 pm

subject: RE: you don't give up, do you?

A nickname, huh? I can respect that. But tit for tat, isn't that what you said? A nickname for a nickname. Last year, people started calling me Skywalker.

———

from: Katydid <getoveryourself@imail.com>
to: Mr.   X
<themanwhofoundyourjournal@imail.com>
date: August 1, 2018 at 12:33 pm
subject: RE: you don't give up, do you?

Skywalker?? You *do* live in your mom's basement, don't you?

———

from: Skywalker
<themanwhofoundyourjournal@imail.com>
to: Katydid <getoveryourself@imail.com>
date: August 1, 2018 at 12:35 pm
subject: RE: you don't give up, do you?

. . .

LOL! Is that what you think of me? That's the thing about nicknames, *Katydid*. You don't usually get any say in the ones that stick.

———

from: Katydid <getoveryourself@imail.com>
    to: Skywalker
<themanwhofoundyourjournal@imail.com>
    date: August 1, 2018 at 12:36 pm
    subject: RE: you don't give up, do you?

You do have a point, as usual. So, tell me, how did you get such an epically nerdy nickname? Gaming? Role play? Spill it, Skywalker.

———

from: Skywalker
<themanwhofoundyourjournal@imail.com>
    to: Katydid <getoveryourself@imail.com>
    date: August 1, 2018 at 12:36 pm
    subject: RE: you don't give up, do you?

. . .

Nope. It's your turn. My ego is already stinging from your swift and brutal judgement.

---

from: Katydid <getoveryourself@imail.com>
   to: Skywalker
<themanwhofoundyourjournal@imail.com>
   date: August 1, 2018 at 12:40 pm
   subject: RE: you don't give up, do you?

My swift and brutal judgment, huh? I don't know how I feel about that.

I'm afraid I'll disappoint you when it comes to nicknames. Mine came about because my mom loved my long, spindly legs when I was a kid. Add that to the fact that I used to hum the same little song over and over whenever I got involved in a project, and she told me I was just like a katydid—a bug that gets its name because its song sounds like it says 'Katy did, Katy didn't' on repeat. Believe me, if I could have picked a different name, I would have. I hated being compared to an icky old bug.

Now. Skywalker. Explain.

Cat

I glanced up from my phone and realized I'd been sitting in a gas station parking lot for the better part of an hour, emailing back and forth with Mr. X. Or, rather, Skywalker. It was good to have a name for him, even if it didn't really suit the image I had been building in my mind.

When he didn't reply right away, I dropped my phone into my purse and turned the key in the ignition. Today was move-in day at The Hut. Since most of my life fit in a few bags in the back of the Jeep, it wouldn't take too long to get myself situated, which might leave me some time to get to know the Huttons. Or at the very least, to explore the area. I navigated myself onto the road and, at the first stoplight, fished my phone out of my purse and put it in the cup holder, so I could see the moment an email came in.

CHAPTER SIXTEEN

LUCAS

She finally had a name. Katydid. A smile grew on my face as I stared at my phone, starting from someplace so deep inside, I'd forgotten it even existed. It wasn't much, and it wasn't as good as knowing her real name, but it was something. I had one more point of information to flesh out the picture I had of her in my head. A little girl with long legs and a song to hum...and a nickname. Katydid.

When she called me out on living in my Mom's basement, I laughed. Her joke hit a little closer to the truth than I was ready to let on. After all, I *was* living in my mother's house—though the circumstances were different than what I'm sure she had in mind. But, so were most of my siblings, which now that I thought about it, maybe made it worse, even though we weren't freeloading. Our story was one of those things you couldn't explain well over text, so I let it be. Maybe one day, when we were face to face, I'd be able to tell her everything.

Explaining my nickname would be difficult. I didn't talk about what happened to me in Afghanistan, the little bit of heroism that had my squad mates calling me Skywalker—a play on my first name and a reference to the fact that I was willing to sacrifice my life for the life of my commanding officer.

My family knew the details of that day. As did my doctors and physical therapists. The people who were there with me knew, of course. Hence the nickname. But now that there wasn't a good reason for the story to be told, I kept my mouth shut on the topic. I had no desire to live through it again—especially in front of anyone who might read the emotion that still strangled me. Better to leave that shit in the past.

That was the beauty of emailing with Katydid—I smiled as I used her name—the anonymity allowed me to talk about things that I wouldn't dare discuss with anyone else. My revelations after waking up in the hospital. The feeling of being the only person in the world with my eyes open. How could I say that to anyone and not have it seem like a slap in the face?

Hey there, little brother, thanks for everything you've done for me. Oh, by the way, have I mentioned that I think you're doing it all wrong? That you've got life backwards? By the way, thanks for all the moral support you've given me since the accident.

Yeah. That just wouldn't have gone over well.

Sharing those thoughts with Katydid was easy. It felt like freedom. And reading her thoughts in return? That was pure bliss. It was too early to tell yet, but I thought I had finally found someone else with her eyes open. We both looked at the world in a way that no one else around us did. Maybe that was why we clicked even when we had never technically met. I wondered if she went back to the coffee shop and stared at the men as they walked in, hoping to discover which one was me. If I was still in Galveston, I'd be in that damn place every day, waiting for her.

And maybe that's why when Wyatt offered to do the new-hire meeting with Cat, I was almost relieved to let him have it. The physical attraction between us was palpable, but my mind belonged to a woman in Texas. Her words had wormed their way into my heart. Maybe, after everything was settled here at The Hut, I'd return to Galveston and meet her face to face.

Today, Cat was moving into the room next to mine. And for as often as I reminded myself that Katydid was here first, my body was quick to remind me that Cat was here now. And so, I waited on the front porch for her to arrive while mentally composing my response to Katydid. The roar of the ocean kept me company and I rubbed at a sore spot in my thigh, cursing under my breath at the pain.

The week had been stressful. Digging through Dad's financial records, Wyatt and I found mistake upon mistake upon mistake. And, for reasons I couldn't quite understand, each new inconsistency we uncovered made Wyatt exponentially more unsettled. When we weren't working on that, I was either obsessing over Cat's arrival, or staying up too late rereading random emails from Katydid, trying to glean as much information as I could. When I woke this morning, I needed to clear my head and took it out on my body, pushing too hard on my run.

My leg gave out within minutes of getting started, but I had too much energy to burn, so I pushed past the first warning sign. And the second. And the third. I only stopped when I realized I couldn't *not* limp and I paid for it all day. I would pay for it tomorrow, too.

A red Jeep sans roof crawled up the driveway and I stood, shielding my eyes against the sun. Cat's red hair flowed in the wind. A smile graced her face. And I swore, I heard strains of her massacring Taylor Swift before she caught me watching and turned off the radio. I limped down the steps as she pulled to a stop.

"Hey there," I said, squinting up at her, smooth as ever.

She smiled as she brushed her hair back off her face. "Hey!" She closed her eyes and tilted her face to the sky. I stared at her profile, the light smattering of freckles across her nose, those full lips, her cheeks pink from the sun. She took a deep breath—which pressed her breasts against the thin fabric of her shirt. I yanked my gaze away just as she opened her eyes. "It's a gorgeous day, isn't it?"

I raised an eyebrow. "You realize the humidity's off the charts, right?"

"True. But the breeze feels amazing." She grinned and I realized Cat must be an optimist if she could find something good in a day with ninety percent humidity. She would fit in with Wyatt and Mom just fine.

"I thought you might need help with your things," I said, then paused and peered into the Jeep. "Though unless you have a truck or something following behind, it looks like I thought wrong." Cat only had a few bags, and I wondered why. People tended to collect stuff as they lived. A vase with memories filling in the crack along the rim. A picture of friends or family. A book with wrinkles along the spine. What happened in Cat's life that she didn't seem to have many, if any, of those kinds of mementos?

"You're more than welcome to help," she said as

she reached into the backseat to produce two giant suitcases. "Who am I to turn down a case of good, old-fashioned chivalry when I find one?" She hefted a bag my way and then hopped out of the Jeep, maneuvering the other out behind her. "Let me just take a minute to put the top up in case it rains."

I propped her luggage on the ground and helped her with the soft top. "You ever take the doors off?" I asked. The Growlers I'd driven overseas were a lot like Jeeps without doors. Getting used to the ground zooming past without anything keeping you safely tucked inside took time. I doubted this little woman was brave enough.

She looked at me like she knew what I was thinking and was all too happy to prove me wrong. "All the time. I didn't today since I kinda needed them with me, now that this place counts as home for a while, you know? It made more sense to transport as actual doors than try to find room in the back."

"You make a good point." I finished zipping up the soft top.

"Usually." She peered around the hood with a look that begged me to say anything different.

I led her toward the house, explaining the intricacies of food and meals. As an employee living in The Hut, she'd have full access to the kitchen, though so did anyone else currently living here, myself included. "It can be a little complicated at first, learning to work around everyone's needs, but we'll find a rhythm."

She stepped onto the porch and paused, turning her face to mine. There was a moment of silent eye contact. I could feel myself glaring down at her, doing 'that thing where I get all intense and glowery' but I had no choice, not with the flood of all things Cat Wallace zinging through my body—her skin, her smile, the light in her hair, her perfume—with Katydid's name chasing along behind, trailing a ribbon of guilt.

Cat blushed and then smiled, and it was the most beautiful thing about her. "How many people live here now?"

I held open the door and gestured for her to enter. "Right now? That's a good question." I started ticking off names in my head, but the number got tangled in my thoughts.

Before I could answer, Wyatt came around the corner with Eli. "What's a good question?" he asked, before his gaze fell on Cat. "Hey! Look who's here!" He greeted her like an old friend and introduced her to our brother who lifted a hand and said, "Hey."

Eli's eyes traveled across Cat's face, down to her shoulders peeking out of her tank top, and right along her perfect breasts. He drank her in, savoring her the way she was built to be savored, and I didn't like it. Not one bit.

"Cat wanted to know how many people live here now," I said to Wyatt while giving Eli a look that meant *back off.*

Wyatt furrowed his brow. "Well, let's see. There's you, Eli, Caleb, and Harlow," he said, holding up fingers as he spoke. "And Mom of course." He added another finger. "Then there's Jimmy and Taylor and Emma." He finished lifting fingers and waggled them my way.

"And now me," said Cat. "So that's nine." She pursed her lips and bobbed her head. "That's a full house. Thank goodness the rooms each have private bathrooms."

"That's nothing." Eli raked a hand through his hair, his gaze darting my way, as if to remind me he didn't need my permission to talk to Cat. "Imagine what it was like when we were kids, back before all the renovations and we only had one bathroom per floor."

The five of us kids each took to our lifestyle in our own unique way. Dealing with the commotion of living in a bed and breakfast came naturally to Wyatt. He adapted to all the hubbub as if he was born for it. Younger me resented the constant change as guests came and went. No matter how much I learned about a person, no matter how much I grew to like them, they were temporary. Here for a week and then gone. Eli learned how to talk to anyone about anything. Caleb got mad. And Harlow took turns either basking in the spotlight or running from it.

Cat laughed, the glimmer in her eyes lighting up the entire room. "I can't. It must have been a madhouse."

Wyatt shrugged. "There was never a dull day, but I'll be honest, I kind of miss it. Now that we're more hotel than B&B, you lose that personal connection with the guests."

"You say that like it's a bad thing," I said, then moved toward the stairs. "I'm gonna show Cat where to put her stuff." I grimaced at the pain in my leg as I guided her up the steps and to her room—located conveniently next to mine—then presented her with two keys, one for the main house and one for the room itself.

"Well," she said, reaching for her suitcase. "Guess it's time for me to get settled in."

"Guess so." My fingers brushed hers when I handed over her bag. Her skin was smooth and cool and all I wanted was more, but my phone weighed heavy in my pocket, a constant reminder of a woman who wasn't mine.

Neither of us moved. After a second, a smile tugged at the corner of her lips and she dropped her eyes to the ground. "Thanks for the help."

"Anytime." Another long pause.

She laughed nervously and slid her key into the lock. "See ya around, Lucas," she said, and with that, she stepped inside and closed the door. I stared after her for a beat, then went into my room, pulled out my laptop, and drafted a reply to Katydid.

CHAPTER SEVENTEEN

FROM: SKYWALKER
<themanwhofoundyourjournal@imail.com>
    to: Katydid <getoveryourself@imail.com>
    date: August 1, 2018 at 2:15 pm
    subject: My nickname

My friends used to tell me I have a hero complex, that I'd sacrifice myself to save the world and apparently, that makes me a lot like Luke Skywalker. I did everything I could to dodge the nickname, but I think that only made it stick harder.

We've been talking about me a lot lately. How are you? Things still crazy?

from: Katydid <getoveryourself@imail.com>
    to: Skywalker
<themanwhofoundyourjournal@imail.com>
    date: August 1, 2018 at 7:45 pm
    subject: RE: My nickname

Sorry it took me so long to reply. It's been a busy day.

I like talking about you. You're the most interesting person I know, and that's saying a lot because I know a purple-haired bodybuilder who just recently came out of the closet. His best friend is a woman who only wears black. Black clothes, black hair, black makeup. She'd say she has a black soul, but she's only being dramatic. They're quite the pair. Draw attention wherever they go. And still, given all that, you're more interesting.

How're things with me? Still crazy. Lots of change.

Earlier you said change sucks and it's easier to settle for the devil you know. I think that's true BEFORE change happens. I think the *prospect* of change sucks. And yes, sometimes the actual change itself sucks, too. (See, there I go again, seeing the opposite side of the coin before I even finish arguing the first side.) Anyway, for me, now that I'm not stuck in the pre-change period, I'm actually having fun.

Yes, the future looks uncertain, but it's also

completely in my hands. It'll be whatever I make of it, and so I'm feeling pretty good about things. The most telling aspect of it all is that I don't miss Nash. Not even one little bit. I don't miss our house. I don't miss our plans for the future. I don't miss having to censor who I am around him.

He hated my purple-haired friend, by the way. The fabulous Christopher Magic lived way too far out of the box for good old conservative and traditional Nash Addington. And before you go drawing mental pictures of me based off my friends, I don't dye my hair or wear crazy makeup. I just like interesting people. That would be my mother's influence, I'm sure. And the part of me that's loyal to my father is the part that let me fall in love with Nash in the first place.

Anyway, I'm rambling and have probably scared you off by yammering away. Tempted to delete this so I'm going to hit send before I do. Tired of censoring myself, so consider this a test.

———

from: Skywalker
<themanwhofoundyourjournal@imail.com>
    to: Katydid <getoveryourself@imail.com>
    date: August 1, 2018 at 8:01 pm
    subject: RE: My nickname

. . .

A purple-haired bodybuilder who came out of the closet to hang out with a goth chick who sounds like Wednesday Addams? I wish you could see me right now. I'm laughing so hard I'm crying. Tell me that's not his real name. Christopher Magic??

Don't ever censor yourself for me. I want you unfiltered. Raw. I want all your thoughts, exactly the way they happen. That's what drew me to you in the first place. Why would I ever want anything less?

CHAPTER EIGHTEEN

Cat

I stared at the words on my screen for five straight minutes, my heart so full, I couldn't stop smiling.

Don't ever censor yourself for me. I want you unfiltered. Raw. I want all your thoughts, exactly the way they happen. That's what drew me to you in the first place. Why would I ever want anything less?

How could my mystery man be so perfect? My Mr. X. My Skywalker. Could he really be everything I needed? Was it possible that I found my soulmate and I'd never even seen him yet? And maybe never would?

That line of thinking felt dangerous, so I dropped my phone onto the bed and crossed the room to stare at myself in the mirror over the dresser.

"You are *not* falling in love with a mysterious stranger," I said to the woman in the reflection. She smirked at me and the look in her eyes said she wasn't as sold on the idea as I was.

The fact that I was thinking about myself in the third person made me realize I needed company and I needed it now. With eight other people in the house, it was silly of me to hide out in my room, even if the view of the ocean dressed in the setting sun was begging me to spend the evening on the balcony, watching the sky catch fire.

I grabbed my keys and shoved my phone in my pocket. If no one was downstairs, maybe I'd take a drive. It wouldn't solve my company problem, but I could always call Chris and rub my fancy new job in his face. Not because I liked holding my good luck over him, but because I thought he liked it when I did.

Laughter met me at the bottom of the stairs and I followed it into the kitchen. There, seated around a large oak dining table, were Wyatt and Lucas, along with two other men and two other women. One of the men I recognized from earlier that afternoon. Eli, I thought. The resemblance between the people in front of me was so strong, it was clear I had stumbled upon a Hutton family gathering. I froze in the doorway and did an abrupt about face, hopeful no one saw me.

Alas, I'd been spotted.

"Cat!" I turned to find Wyatt waving me over, a giant smile on his sun-kissed face.

"Hey." I lifted a hand. "I'm sorry to interrupt..."

"Don't be silly. Sit. Join us." Wyatt pointed to an empty chair beside Lucas, who was busy checking his phone. "I told you, when you work for the Huttons, you're family. That's not just a line I fed you so you'd sign away your life to us." The family met the statement with varying degrees of acceptance, but they all nodded in agreement.

An older woman with a long, red braid, streaked with gray but still lush and beautiful, tracked me as I crossed the room. Her face was worn, but her eyes were bright. "Is this the mystical Cat Wallace I've been hearing about?"

Mystical? What in the world had I done to earn an adjective like that? I held out my hands sheepishly. "None other."

A smile even friendlier than Wyatt's broke across her face. "Fantastic! Have a seat. It's killing me that we haven't chatted yet. I always spend some time with our new hires, especially the ones that choose to stay with us. Rebecca Hutton, by the way," she finished as I sat.

"It's a pleasure." I couldn't help but glance at Lucas who was staring at me strangely, eyes narrowed, brow crinkled. Such a change from his friendly demeanor this afternoon. Unsettled, I gave my attention back to

Rebecca. "Really, it is. I've heard so much about you from Wyatt and Lucas." Another glance his way. Our eyes met and my heart stopped. My stomach flipped. All semblance of coherence stuttered away, and I stammered out the rest of my sentence to Rebecca. What was it about this man that had me unable to think straight? Thankfully, Wyatt spoke, stealing my attention, and my thoughts settled into something that almost made sense.

"You met Eli this afternoon," he said, indicating the brown-haired man from earlier. Eli lifted a hand. "And that handsome blonde devil over there is Caleb. And this here is our delicate flower of a sister, Harlow."

Caleb lifted a hand and Harlow punched Wyatt in the arm. "See?" he asked, rubbing his shoulder while Harlow rolled her eyes.

Before I knew what happened, I had a drink in my hand and enough conversation to never feel lonely again. The family was boisterous and friendly, and I got the distinct impression they were catching up with each other rather than having a regular conversation. That afternoon, Wyatt had mentioned they were all staying in rooms upstairs, well, all of them except for him, and I wondered at the reason. Surely, they didn't all still live there? Had I interrupted a family reunion?

They laughed and told stories of growing up, taking the time to explain inside jokes so I could laugh right along with them. It was surreal, sitting around a table this big with a family this lively. It was the perfect juxtaposition of my stoic dinners with Dad and my less than formal meals with Mom. In a matter of hours, I felt right at home.

Throughout it all, Lucas had my attention. When I thought he wasn't looking, I would glance his way, only to find him watching me. I wanted to memorize the angle of his jaw, the quirk of his lips. Even the sheen of blonde hair on his tan forearm was mesmerizing. His voice sent my stomach into a tizzy and quite suddenly, it was all a little more than I could stand.

My mere presence seemed to make him tense, though that could just as easily be that I had the same effect on him as he did on me. Or, it could be my ego talking, but I had a pretty good track record when it came to reading people. Although, considering recent events, one could argue that I wasn't as good at it as I thought, seeing as my fiancé had been cheating on me and I never had the slightest suspicion. Which was the thought that brought me crashing right back down to earth.

I didn't have room in my life for men right now and between Skywalker and Lucas, I had enough drama going on that the Magic Man himself would be proud. I giggled to myself, drawing a strange look from Lucas. Maybe it was time I stopped drinking whatever it was

Eli kept pouring. The concoction was tasty enough that it went down easily, but I was starting to think these colorful little drinks packed quite a punch. I slid my glass away. Rebecca caught my eye, made a face that said she understood, and did the same.

"Hey..." Wyatt leaned forward to catch my attention. "Do you have clients tomorrow? She doesn't have clients tomorrow, does she Mom?"

The entire table erupted in laughter, myself included. He sounded like a little boy, asking his mother if a friend could sleep over.

Wyatt looked around, confused. "What?"

"Aren't you the manager?" Caleb asked. "Shouldn't you be the one to know without having to ask Mom?"

Wyatt waved away the question. "Yes, I should know, but with all you guys getting your noses into my stuff, I've lost track. Besides, these are strong." And he, too, pushed his glass away.

I shook my head. "I don't have clients tomorrow because, if I remember correctly, the *manager* wanted to give me time to settle in before he put me to work."

There was more laughter. "She's going to fit in well around here," Harlow said, and everyone agreed.

Wyatt waited for the table to quiet down with a good-natured look on his face. "*Anyway,*" he said to me, "we're going out on the boat tomorrow. You should come."

I couldn't help it, I glanced at Lucas. He glared at me, his brow knit together and I flinched. That settled it. Obviously, I was not as good at reading people as I thought. The intense attraction between us was not mutual. And double obviously, Lucas did not want me to butt in on their little family gathering.

"See!" Wyatt pointed a finger at Lucas. "That. Right there. The super intense glowery thing. You're doing it, brother." He turned to me. "I promise you, whatever he's thinking is less terrifying than it looks."

Lucas glanced at his brother, then turned back to me. Maybe I was less skilled than my mother when it came to reading facial cues and maybe I wasn't, but I swore, the twist in his lips when he turned to Wyatt said, 'that's what you think.'

CHAPTER NINETEEN

CAT

The sun burned down on us, heat baking the sand beneath our feet as we crossed from The Hut to the dock—a long line of scorched wood, bleached almost white with time, extending into clear blue water. Harlow scurried ahead while the rest of us followed behind, picking up her bare feet with each step and wincing at the heat.

"Seattle has made you weak," Eli said to her as he strolled onto the dock.

"Yeah, well, you're still the same old you," Harlow replied with a toss of her hair and a glint in her eye.

Caleb leaned into Eli and fake whispered, "She's calling you an asshole."

The Huttons tossed sarcasm around like candy, giving as good as they got. I watched as they climbed onto a large boat, never breaking the flow of conversation. Lucas followed his siblings, then turned and offered me his hand. When his skin touched mine, that rolling thunder feeling of excitement soared through me, but I swallowed it down.

"Thank you," I said, glancing his way.

"No problem." He smiled and I smiled and he stared and I stared and Wyatt burst out laughing, breaking the spell as he dropped a hand on Lucas' shoulder.

"Keep it professional now," he said, then went to work helping Caleb with ropes and anchors and all kinds of nautical stuff that made little sense to me.

I blushed, but Lucas caught my eye and winked. Last night, I thought he hated me. Today, it looked like we were going to be friends. If he didn't slow down with the mood swings, I was going to get whiplash.

Caleb started the boat and navigated us away from the dock, the rumble of the engine and the smell of gasoline mixing with the briny air. Despite the heat, the weather was perfect. I stared out to sea, the wind blowing through my hair. It was vast and beautiful, and peace settled into my heart, lightening the load on my shoulders.

How did people manage to spend their entire lives

blocked off from nature? I was born to be outside. Healing hid in the wind, the sound of the birds, the lap of water against the boat. My mind turned to Skywalker, certain he would find a way to turn my clumsy thought into poetry. He would understand something I could only feel and transform those feelings into words I would read over and over and over again, sighing and smiling and content.

I almost grabbed my phone to snap a picture for him, but I looked up to find Lucas watching me. When my gaze brushed his, he grinned and then turned his attention to Eli, who was halfway through a story about the time Harlow found a litter of abandoned kittens and brought them home in the basket on her bike. I put my phone away.

"I thought Dad was gonna lose his mind," Eli said, "but you and Mom bottle fed those things and basically brought them back from the dead. You remember?"

Harlow gathered her hair into a ponytail and wrapped a hair tie around it. "Oh, I remember. I wanted to keep one so badly. But Dad put his foot down."

"He used the possibility of guests with allergies as his foolproof logic for why he was right and you were wrong, didn't he?" Eli asked. A muscle in his jaw ticked and he ran a hand through his hair.

Harlow nodded. "He did."

"He had a point," Caleb countered.

Eli rolled his eyes. "He also had a God complex."

"No arguing there." Caleb let out a long breath and gave his attention back to the water.

Silence fell between the siblings and smiles faded from faces. I dropped my gaze to my lap, fiddling with the hem of my coverup. It appeared we had stumbled out of pleasant memories and into the kind that latched on to feet and ankles and pulled my new friends downward, quicksand dragging them into an abyss. The siblings sunk in on themselves and I wondered what, if anything, I should say.

"Our dad passed away last month," Lucas explained, his voice tense. "It's why we're all here. Back in the Keys. Mom needs our help." His jaw ticked like Eli's and something glinted in his eyes, something dark and terrible. There was more to this story and I wasn't sure I wanted to hear it.

"I'm sorry to hear that," I said.

"Don't be." Eli stared at the horizon. "We're not."

"Eli!" Harlow admonished, her eyes going wide as she looked from him to me and back again.

"What?" Eli held out his hands then let them drop. "I'm just saying what we're all thinking. Besides, it's better if Cat hears it from us, rather than anyone else."

Lucas explained, obviously giving me only as much

as I needed to understand. Burke Hutton had been a good father...until he wasn't.

He started making money, and then started drinking, proceeding to ruin the family he'd worked so hard to build. The kids scattered as soon as they could, hurt and confused and wearing the kind of scars that rip through a heart and soul—the kind that come when love was given and then taken away without reason or explanation. The kind that leaves you wondering what would make someone wonderful stop looking at you like the whole damn world lived in your eyes. I sucked in my lips and sent a silent *fuck you* to Nash.

"So, yeah," Wyatt said. "How about we stop depressing Cat and focus on where we are instead of where we've been?" He gestured toward the front of the boat as Caleb navigated us into a cove filled with the bluest water I had ever seen. White sand glistened on the beach as waves lapped against the shore. Palm trees drooped, their fronds swaying in the breeze.

I gaped at the view and the Huttons chuckled at my awestruck expression. Caleb killed the engine and before the boat had drifted to a stop, Wyatt yanked his shirt over his head and dove into the water. He broke the surface, shaking water out of his hair, droplets sparkling in the sun. "What are you waiting for? Get in here!"

Eli and Caleb followed suit, removing shirts and

jumping in. Caleb dropped in feet first while Eli tucked into a ball and landed next to Wyatt, splashing water in his brother's face. Lucas stood and pulled his shirt over his head, exposing a muscular torso with scars speckled along his side, disappearing into his swim trunks, and reappearing on one leg.

He held out his hand and I dragged my gaze up to his face. "You coming?" he asked. He had caught me staring at the scars, but didn't call me on it. He didn't explain either, and we didn't know each other well enough for me to ask, even though I wanted to.

"Of course I'm coming," I said. "Life is made for the doers and the movers." I placed my hand in his and a flicker of something flashed across his face. I wasn't sure what it was, but like everything he did, it overwhelmed me and made me want more at the same time I just wished I could take one complete breath.

He helped me stand, then removed his hand from mine. "I agree one hundred percent."

Lucas caught my gaze and raised an eyebrow, before diving off the side of the boat, disappearing under the water, then reappearing with a shake of his head. He slicked his hair back from his face, then crooked a finger at me, beckoning for me to follow.

I took a moment to appreciate the view in the cove and the brothers horse-playing before dropping in. The cool water shocked my warm skin. The rush of bubbles danced across my face, muffling my hearing. I stayed under as my hair floated around me, a moment of weightless solitude, then broke the surface and found myself face to face with Lucas.

"Hi," he said.

"Hi," I replied, and somehow the moment felt more real than anything I'd experienced to date.

We played in the water like children, splashing and swimming and racing and teasing. We snorkeled and skied, both of which I'd never done before. Lucas proved to be a patient and eloquent teacher. While I started both endeavors feeling nervous, by the time we finished, I was confident in my ability not to die. When we got tired, we climbed back into the boat. The men shook their hair out next to their sister, spraying her with water while she gasped and shrieked and goosebumps pebbled along her arms.

We ate a simple lunch and I stretched out next to Lucas as the salt dried on our skin. We chatted easily, the strange tension between us fading, until my curiosity got the better of me. "Where did these come from?" I asked, lightly running a finger along one of the many scars on his torso.

He flinched away from my touch, his face darkening as he pushed into a sitting position.

"I'm sorry," I said. "It's none of my business."

"It really isn't." His voice was clipped and his gaze

was distant, as if the hours we'd spent building a friendship today hadn't happened at all.

I felt myself go red from head to toe and sat up, tucking my knees to my chest while I leaned back on my hands and stared at the horizon. His reaction embarrassed me. Again, apparently I'd misjudged how he felt about me. Or, maybe I'd overstepped the boundaries of friendship. Whatever injury caused those scars must still ache beneath the surface. I shouldn't have asked.

"Hey." Lucas shifted closer to me. "I'm sorry," he said as bumped his shoulder against mine. "I don't like talking about it, is all."

"I get it. It's none of my business." I tossed him a smile.

A breeze whispered in his hair and his eyes—as blue as the water yet more vibrant—caught mine. He stared, his gaze steady. "No. You're fine, Cat. I overreacted."

I swallowed hard, my lips parting while that still-small voice stood up inside me and roared: *THIS!*

"What? Lucas overreacted?" Caleb plopped down next to us and as much as I liked the guy, I wanted him to go away because whatever that voice inside me had to say disappeared the moment he arrived. "Hey! Did you guys hear that? Lucas overreacted about something!"

Lucas rolled his eyes as Wyatt joined us. "Let me guess," Wyatt said to me. "You asked about his scars."

Horrified by the direction the conversation was headed, I looked for something, *anything* to say to diffuse the situation. If Lucas didn't want to talk about what happened to him, the last thing I wanted was for his brother to tease him into sharing. I stammered, but Lucas interrupted.

"Did you know I'm a Marine?" he asked me.

I shook my head. "I didn't." Though that bit of information explained so much about him, the intensity and harsh demeanor that juxtaposed his good nature.

Lucas took a long breath in and let it out. "Last year, in Afghanistan, a series of bombs ended my career."

"Almost ended his life." Wyatt smiled at his brother, a mixture of pride and sadness softening his eyes.

Caleb leaned in. "It *did* end his life. He actually was dead for two minutes and it was touch and go for a while after that. Mom was beside herself. We all were."

A rush started in my belly and roared through my head as I absorbed the information. "He died last year?" I stared at Lucas with wide eyes while Skywalker's words screamed at me.

I died last year. I came back, obviously. And I

wasn't dead long. But there were times, especially at first, that I wished I'd stayed wherever it was I went...

"Yep. But Lucas here is a fighter..."

...Coming back was hard. It changed everything. I realized how fragile we all are. I realized that so much of what we cherish means nothing in the end. I was alone through a lot of my recovery and I kept wondering why I was fighting so hard. Why battle through it all when I had nothing to battle for...?

"...he made it back to us and earned himself one hell of a nickname."

My heart pounded its way up my throat. Could it be? Was this him? Were Lucas and Skywalker somehow the same person? That couldn't be possible. Skywalker was in Galveston.

Wasn't he?

"Enough with the nickname already." Lucas tried to look annoyed, but he was too busy cataloging my reaction. His eyes flicked around my face. He licked his lips. Tilted his head.

His words came to me as if I was still underwater. They were heavy and thick, distorted and full of echoes. *I swear to God, if they call him Skywalker...*

"Oh, come on." Wyatt grinned. "How can you not love being called the Bionic Man?"

"Wait." Eli appeared over Wyatt's shoulder. "I thought we called him Robocop."

While the brothers laughed and the conversation moved on, I fought my breath back under control. As they explained his injuries, his stay in a hospital in Germany, and his subsequent honorable discharge, I hid a minor mental breakdown.

How dumb was I? How could I have thought Lucas was Skywalker, even for a second? Skywalker was in Texas, not Florida. Skywalker was open and poetic, while Lucas was closed and confusing and intense. The only thing the two men had in common was the fact that they died sometime last year.

That, and...

...well...

...me.

CHAPTER TWENTY

C<small>AT</small>

We returned home later that night, sunburned and exhausted. I hauled my tired body upstairs and let myself into my room, replaying bits and pieces of the day with the Huttons. Harlow's confidence with her brothers. Eli's easy conversation. Caleb's hulking strength. Wyatt's constant smile.

And then there was Lucas...

I had never known someone as intense as that man. Friendly one minute. Withdrawn the next. Though, perhaps, given what I had learned about what happened to him in Afghanistan, I should cut the man some slack. An experience like that didn't just leave scars on the body. His soul had to be still healing as well.

My skin itched with dried saltwater, and sand had made its way into places I hadn't known existed until today. After a long shower, I pulled on a clean pair of shorts and a tank top and plopped into bed.

Lately, I'd been wondering more and more about what Skywalker looked like. Did he have the same broad shoulders and bronze skin as Lucas? Or was he more refined, less warrior-like? Did his wisdom show in his eyes? Did he walk around radiating an inner light that put people at ease? Or did his deep thoughts make him unnerving in that way intelligent people sometimes have?

In my mind, I started putting together a Pinterest board of features that might belong to Skywalker. I focused on the eyes, strong and piercing, with a quick intelligence glimmering in his gaze. Then his shoulders, broad and capable of holding me up when I fell down.

I leaned back in my bed, burrowing my head into a pillow, and let my mind wander around my favorite parts of a masculine body, formulating the perfect image of my mystery man. As the picture grew clearer, I remembered Skywalker's note in my journal:

If I could spend one night with you, I would trace my

fingers along your body as you quivered beneath me. I would taste you and tease you, gripping your waist while you arched your back. I would run my hands along your thighs, lower my face, and lick and suck until you screamed my name. You'd forget the world in your ecstasy and then I'd make love to you while you came and came and came.

I would ruin you for any other man, but you would have all the words you could possibly need to describe the sensation. There would be no more gray and ash and boredom. There would be heat so vibrant, the world would catch fire. Your body would be my temple and I would be your savior and you would never feel like an obligation again.

Much to my immense surprise, my numb lower regions sputtered to life. I closed my eyes and slid a hand down my stomach, imagining the coarse skin of a man's hand brushing across my most sensitive parts.

...lower...

...lower...

...lower...

My lips parted and I sighed as my body responded with a definitive *hell yes*! Hope bloomed in my chest. We might actually get somewhere tonight! I settled deeper into my bed, letting my mind run away with the perfect image of a man, one who would satisfy every secret desire I'd ever had. Blonde hair and tan skin, that was a given. A strong torso, something powerful and hard.

I imagined trailing my fingers across his muscled flesh and smiled as I traced one of the scars mottling his hips...

My eyes flew open and the heat building in my core simmered away. I wasn't thinking about Skywalker anymore. Those scars belonged to Lucas!

That was one hundred percent unacceptable. I couldn't touch myself, knowing he was just on the other side of the wall...

Maybe stretched out in his bed...

Maybe wearing nothing but a pair of gray sweatpants...

Or maybe wearing nothing at all...

And just like that, the fire flared hotter than it had in the last year or two. Or three. Or maybe ever before.

I settled back into my bed, letting my hands travel over my body, urging my mental image of Skywalker away from Lucas. I was wrong to choose a blonde. That's where things went off track. With the hair.

I envisioned dark hair, with sharp green eyes that missed nothing. A full beard. Maybe a tattoo. No...two tattoos. One on his arm and one on his back.

Perfect.

I urged my body forward, testing new waters with my mysterious stranger and his strong, proud cock, capable of the most illicit torture. I imagined him dominating me, throwing me to the bed and ravaging my body, then inviting me on top to take it slow and ride out wave after wave of pleasure at my leisure.

My body responded to the image and I kept my fingers busy, teasing and playing, drawing up feeling and sensation where I thought none would ever exist again. In the other room, I heard the rattle of Lucas' headboard against our shared wall as he climbed into bed. A tense moan slipped past my clenched teeth.

He was right there.

So close.

Nothing but drywall separating us.

And maybe he was touching himself, too...

And that was the end of that.

I slid my hand out of my underwear and pushed myself into a sitting position. What, in the name of everything holy, was I doing? Lucas was hot, no doubt. And he would be perfect masturbation fodder, if I wasn't already trying to think about someone else. Someone who had been so kind to me, so sweet and sincere.

Oh God! What if I had managed to finish? Talk about awkward. The one time in how many years I managed to find an orgasm, and it was only after imagining Lucas Hutton touching himself.

Shame burned in my cheeks and I glanced at the

wall separating us, as if he could somehow know what had almost happened in my room. Blowing a puff of air past my lips, I stood and paced my small room, suddenly filled with frustrated energy. I had been so close. So. Close.

I needed to move, and a strenuous yoga session sounded almost mandatory at the moment. I wouldn't get the physical release I needed, but maybe I could exhaust myself enough to fall asleep without having to think about what almost just happened.

The thought of yoga on the balcony appealed to me, but Lucas had spent a good portion of last night out on his. The worst possible thing I could have to face right now was...well...him. My poker face wasn't strong enough to try and pull off small talk after what just happened. The moment he looked at me, I would melt into a pile of red-hot embarrassment, possibly blurting out an admission of wrongdoing on my way down.

Instead of the balcony, I opted for a trip to the beach. I could stretch my mat out on the sand and enjoy feeling small beside the vast sea. Confident I had a solid plan on my hands, I grabbed my mat and my keys and stepped into the hallway...

...and ran straight into Lucas.

Literally.

"Whoa," he said, gripping my shoulders as my face rebounded off his rock-hard chest. "You good?"

No. I wasn't good. Not at all. Every second of the last fifteen minutes was the stuff of nightmares.

"Oh, sure," I replied, in what I hoped was my breeziest voice. "Just headed out for some yoga." I hefted my mat, presenting it as evidence that everything was perfectly normal and as it should be. When my eyes met his, I felt my cheeks go hot. I forced a smile, totally aware I must look slightly maniacal. "What about you? You good?"

Lucas looked like he couldn't decide if the conversation was more hilarious or confusing, though maybe it was an equal blend of both. "Just heading out for a run." He lifted a foot, highlighting a running shoe, gently mocking my gesture with the mat. "Walk with me?"

"Uh..." I glanced at my door, as if I could find an excuse to run away conveniently taped there. "I just... you know...uh...sure."

"What is it with you?" Lucas asked on a laugh. "You're acting like I caught you at something red-handed."

I waved away his statement, valiantly ignoring the innuendo I could never live down. "Oh no." I tossed my head back and laughed, the coolest cucumber in all the world. "Just figured you might be sick of me by now."

Lucas wrapped a friendly arm around my shoulder and I couldn't help it. I inhaled, breathing him in as if I could lock it in my memory and draw upon it the next time I needed...inspiration.

Lucas peered down at me, one eyebrow raised in question. "Did you just sniff me?"

"Uhh...no?"

He shook his head, but didn't remove his arm. In fact, and this totally could have been my imagination, but it felt like he pulled me closer. "You're one strange chick, Cat," he said when we reached the bottom of the stairs.

And with that, he leaned down, buried his nose in my hair and took a deep breath.

"Hey! Who's weird now?" I asked, as I pulled out from under his arm.

Lucas never broke his stride. "Still you," he called over his shoulder, heading toward the door. "You coming?"

His question sent another blush flaring across my cheeks because no. If tonight was any indication, I would never get to come again.

CHAPTER TWENTY-ONE

FROM: KATYDID <GETOVERYOURSELF@IMAIL.COM>
to: Skywalker
<themanwhofoundyourjournal@imail.com>
date: August 3, 2018 at 9:45 pm
subject: deep thoughts

I thought about you a lot yesterday. I met some people I
think you would like, people I really think I like.
They're open and kind and caring and...intense.
Hanging out with them has made me realize how difficult it is to get to know someone. And I mean, really get
to know them. In order to get to who anyone really is,
you have to creep past their defenses, gaining trust
along the way until they finally lower their guard and
let you in.

We all put up fronts, these pleasant façades that we wear for different people. We have one for strangers, one for acquaintances, one for people we want to impress. How are we ever supposed to know if we're dealing with the façade, or if we've finally met the real person?

What if the façade never drops? Are we always walking around, being someone less than true to ourselves in order to be what we think other people want?

Or worse, what happens when that façade doesn't drop until you're so deeply involved in a relationship that you can't remember what life was like without it? The mask drops and you realize the person you thought you knew doesn't exist. Instead, you're tangled up with this funhouse mirror version of someone you've dedicated your life to. I think that's what happened with Nash. I thought I knew him. Turned out, I only knew the parts of him I chose to see.

You and I didn't go through that song and dance of getting to know each other. Of figuring out if we liked each other. Of wondering what the other one is thinking.

We just dove right in.

Or rather, you just dove right in. (Have I mentioned that I'll never let you forget that you read my journal??)

I've only gotten bits and pieces of you and your life, but huge glimpses at how you see the world. And so, while I feel this deep connection and appreciation for you because I can—and do!—tell you everything I'm thinking, we're still strangers.

While we go on and on about what we're thinking and feeling, we haven't even begun to talk about our daily lives. Our family. Our names.

We're still wearing masks. Afraid to take them off, even when we've never met face to face.

And maybe I like it that way because I'm scared. After Nash, maybe I'm not ready for anything more than a pleasant façade. Maybe I just want to daydream about you being perfect so I don't have to worry about what happens when the mask comes off.

This isn't a very pleasant email, but I'm swimming through some not so pleasant thoughts.

Again, considering deleting it and trying to get some sleep. Maybe I'll feel better in the morning and can save you from whatever bad mood I'm currently in.

But. You told me not to censor myself, so here you go.

I hit send and stared at the wall, listening to Lucas moving around in his room. Faint thumps of his feet against the floor. The hiss of the sliding door opening to the balcony and then sliding closed again. Outside, the stars shone over the water and the moon hung full and luminous in the sky. Inside, I regretted sending that email. It asked too much of a man who had done nothing but try and make me feel beautiful from the moment he met me.

Except we hadn't actually met, so maybe I was being too hard on myself.

The sleep I knew I needed was a long way away. And so, rather than lay in bed and stew in my prickly thoughts, I slid open my door and stepped onto the balcony. Lucas glared at his phone, the screen illuminating his face as he read. Whatever he was seeing wasn't making him happy, though with Lucas, it was hard to tell just what he was feeling at any given moment. He looked up as I sat in my chair and kicked my feet up on the railing.

"Hey," he said as he locked his phone and slipped it into his pocket. "Can't sleep?"

I shook my head and leaned back in my chair. "Haven't tried yet." I swiveled my head to meet his gaze. "But it feels like it's going to be one of those nights, you know?"

"Believe me. I know." Lucas smiled sadly. We sat silently as the ocean whispered and roared beneath us. Lost in our thoughts. Comfortably together yet alone, side by side on twin balconies, separated by some wrought iron and an inch of space.

"So how long are you...?" I began at the same time he asked, "Are you liking it...?"

We laughed and I gestured. "You first."

"I was just going to ask if you like it here," he said.

"I do," I replied with a slight nod. The room was small but comfortable. The company was new yet oddly familiar. And the job itself was better than I could have ever hoped for.

"Wow." Lucas sat back in his chair. "With a glowing endorsement like that, I won't hesitate to tell Wyatt he won't have to worry about you leaving."

I laughed lightly as I counted the stars. When I was younger, I used to worry about, well, everything. School. Grades. Friends. The color of my hair. When my anxiety was at its worst, my mom would take me out on the porch. She'd point at the stars, whispering their names to me.

These have been here for more years than you can understand, she'd say. *And no matter how bad your grades are, they'll still be here tomorrow.*

At first, I didn't understand, or really, I thought she was the one who didn't understand. How could a silly old star have anything to do with whatever tragedy was befalling me? The older I got, the more the lesson she'd been trying to teach me came into focus. And now, whenever life got too big, I came outside and stared at the things that had always been here and would still be here tomorrow. And the day after. And the day after that. The sun. The sky. The water. The stars.

"Sorry," I said to Lucas. "I'm just stuck in my head or something. I really love it here." I gave him my attention and a sad smile.

"I'm glad to hear that." It was hard to see his face in the low light, but maybe that was for the best. Maybe that meant he couldn't see mine and I could let down my mask a little and stop pretending to be anyone but me.

"I'm here," he said. "If you need to talk, I'll listen."

Maybe it was the mood I was in. Maybe it was the darkness separating us. Maybe it was thinking about my mom. Maybe it was because he'd shared his tragedy with me yesterday. Whatever the reason, I felt comfortable enough to continue.

"Life's been weird these past few months. I don't typically let things get to me, but...I don't know. I'm feeling unsettled tonight, I guess."

Lucas nodded but didn't say anything and we listened as soft chords from a guitar thrummed somewhere below us. The music threaded through the song of the ocean and I closed my eyes and took it all in. This place was truly paradise.

"It's hard to find our place when it feels like the

sand keeps shifting beneath our feet." Lucas spoke so softly, he could have been speaking to himself. "Growing up here, when I was little, man, it was something. We all just lived excited, all the time. Mom and Dad were thrilled over how well the business was doing, how fast it was growing. I had a place and a purpose. Then Dad started drinking and boom. Everything mutated. What was happy became hard. What was right became wrong."

His words conjured up images of a little boy losing his footing, unsure of how he fit into a world that used to feel so certain. My heart broke for him. In my head, I watched him grow into a man, determined to find his path. A man who needed to prove his worth so much, he became a Marine. And then, in a senseless act of violence, he lost that, too. In comparison, my complaints seemed trivial. My fiancé cheated. I chose to leave. The end.

I took a breath. "Yeah, I guess I really don't have a whole lot of reason to complain."

Lucas shifted, crossing his ankle over his knee and turning so he could look straight at me. "I don't know. New city. New job. You're living in a hotel. That sounds like some shifting sand to me."

"A little. But nothing that ground-breaking. I left my fiancé. Had to stay with my mom. She's doing this thing where she lives in an RV." I shrugged, never sure if I was proud of my mom for the way she lived or if I was embarrassed. "She set out when I was in middle school. To see the world."

"Without you?" I could hear the unspoken question in Lucas' voice. Everyone who heard my story expected the drama of abandonment and the tragedy of loss. And sure, I was upset and confused at first, but if you knew my mom, the decision only made sense.

"Yeah. Without me. I went to live with my dad, which was fine. I mean, it was a change, because he was all rules and structure where my mom..." I searched for words to describe my mother's free spirit.

"Is the kind of woman who lives in an RV?"

"Exactly."

"How old where you when she took off?"

"I wouldn't exactly call it taking off..." I explained the day she sat twelve-year-old me down and informed me that I'd be moving in with my dad. "She was very up front about it. I mean, I was bitter for a bit, but I was almost a teenager, so what wasn't I bitter about?"

Lucas stared up at the sky before responding. "Is that why you're here now instead of staying with her? Still bitter?"

"Oh, God." I let my legs drop off the railing. "Is that how I seem to you? Believe me, no bitterness here. I made peace with my mom and her nomadic ways a long time ago. She doesn't have room for me in the RV.

She's all too happy to make room, but there are only so many nights a person can spend on a bed that moonlights as a table."

Lucas laughed and the conversation moved on. We talked about his days as a Marine and I was duly impressed by what he willingly put himself through to carve out his place in the world. We talked about my life as a masseuse and my plans for the future. "What about you?" I asked, after explaining my desire to one day open my own wellness spa. "What does the future hold for Lucas Hutton?"

He turned his gaze out to the water and frowned. "That's the thing," he said. "I'm still standing in quicksand. Have been ever since I got hurt. Nothing seems to fit. Mom wants me to settle in here." He shrugged. "Maybe this is where I belong." His eyes settled on mine and I couldn't be sure he was talking about the Hut anymore.

"Maybe it is." I wasn't sure I was talking about the Hut anymore, either. I stifled a massive yawn. "Wow. Excuse me." I swiped at my eyes and rubbed my face as Lucas stood.

"Yeah, it's about that time, isn't it?" We said our goodnights and stepped into our respective rooms. As I stretched out in bed, I realized the melancholy from earlier was gone. I fell asleep listening to the waves and wondering about Lucas.

CHAPTER TWENTY-TWO

Lucas

Fire licked up my leg. My pants melted into my skin. Blood dripped into my eyes and the sky burned. Smoke crawled down my throat, raking its clawed fingers across my lungs, and sweat trailed like ice down my spine. In the distance, my commanding officer disappeared in another blast. His body flew through the air, limp. He hit the ground and tumbled bonelessly. I heaved myself onto my hands and my one good knee, and crawled to him, dragging my useless leg behind me.

I screamed without sound. His name lost amongst the chaos.

Rock and debris embedded in my hands and knees

while I fought my way to his wasted body. His eyes stared without seeing, but his chest lifted and fell, and then, I saw nothing but darkness and felt nothing but pain as I burned and burned and burned.

Sweat drenched my body. I threw the covers off and sat up, shivering as I dropped my head into my palms. I ran a shaking hand into my hair and let out a breath. There are things we see and experience that can't be undone. That day in the desert was one of them. It proved to me the brutal fragility of life. We all believe the people we love and the things we have will be with us for the rest of forever. All of it an illusion, a house of cards built on shifting sands.

Everything could change in the space of a second. Order succumbed to chaos. Hope gave way to fear. Some of us fight our way back out again, smoothing all the broken bits into something resembling who we used to be. Some of us stay submerged forever.

Over the last year, I fought myself out of the wreckage left by that horrendous night in Afghanistan. There were times when the urge to kill myself felt stronger than I was—the easiest way to end my torment. But I refused to give in to those dark thoughts, even though the memories of that night clung to me like an anchor tied around my waist.

The doctors assured me the dreams would fade as I healed. They didn't. The more time I spent with doctors, the more I wondered how much they really knew anyway. It wasn't too long ago they believed in leeches and bloodletting as cures to just about anything. How long before today's technological breakthroughs sounded more like voodoo than medicine?

I swung my legs off the edge of the bed, appreciating the plush carpet between my toes. Time to find happier topics. I wasn't surprised when my mind turned to Cat.

My reaction when she asked about my scars the other day surprised me. I thought I'd healed enough that I could talk about that night without bristling. I was wrong. Cat was the first non-family or military person to ask me about them and I wasn't prepared for how hard it was to explain.

Even telling Katydid in an email hadn't come close to looking Cat in the eyes while I told her what happened to me. With Katydid, I had time to edit my words, to smooth over the parts I didn't want to talk about. I didn't have to worry about my tone of voice or the panic in my eyes. I took hours to groom my story and make it sound like I'd come through it without breaking. The reality of staring Cat in the face, of knowing she could see every emotion I felt as I was feeling it, watching the shock and pity in her eyes...that was an entirely different experience.

It wasn't pleasant, though I was probably better for it and I was glad she knew.

Kind of.

Maybe.

I wasn't sure.

I stood and stretched, rubbing at the sore spot in my neck and shaking out my thigh before heading to the bathroom to splash cold water on my face. The clock on my phone read five forty-five, too early to be up, but too late to go to bed. I brushed my teeth and got dressed, then quietly slid open the patio door and watched the day slowly appear.

As the sun blazed into existence, I opened my phone and reread the email from Katydid, worrying about the somber tone. It wasn't like her. Outside of Wyatt, she was the most positive person I knew and I admired that about her. Maybe it was a skill she had honed over the years, or maybe she took time to culti-vate her words to me in the same way I did for her, putting her best foot forward without having to worry about tone and facial expression or struggling to find the right words face to face.

She said we just dove right into our relationship, that we skipped the awkward part where we got to know each other. I wasn't so sure she was right. We were still very much strangers. We were still wearing masks.

Two weeks passed and the nightmares came and went. This morning, I overslept and hurried through getting ready, though I wasn't sure why. I had nowhere to be other than here, and Wyatt and I would get to work when it felt natural. Old habits, I guess. Once a Marine, always a Marine. I would never feel good about sleeping in again.

The kitchen was the happening place to be by the time I got downstairs. Cat sat at the table, hunched over her phone while scraping a spoon around a bowl of cereal. Taylor and Emma leaned against the counter, sipping coffee and chatting about their upcoming days. Caleb hovered over a pan of scrambled eggs, and Harlow sat across from Cat, strumming a wandering tune on her guitar, pausing from time to time to jot something down in a notebook open on the table. I paused in the doorway and Cat looked up. Her hair was piled messily on top of her head, and tan legs barely covered by tiny shorts crossed elegantly under the table. She gave me a knowing look as I took in the crowded area.

"Welcome to the party," she said as I snagged the seat next to her. Caleb offered me some eggs, claiming he made too much, which I happily accepted. His eyes were notoriously bigger than his stomach.

"Whatcha studying so closely?" I asked, peering at the screen on Cat's phone.

She made a show of covering it up. "Hey! No peeking!" She gave me a look before shrugging and showing me what she'd hidden: a map of the surrounding area. "I want to explore this evening, but I hate getting lost, so I'm trying to get an idea of where to go. I've been here almost two weeks and only know how to get to the store and to my mom's."

"Ahh...the adventure of exploring a new area by planning out all your destinations in advance." I scooped a healthy bite of eggs into my mouth and chewed while Cat sputtered a series of excuses. I placed a finger over her lips and her eyes went wide. "Tell you what," I said. "I'll show you around, but I get to drive the Jeep."

She removed my finger from her lips and gave me a playful look. "So that's how you think it works, huh? Now that we're friends, you just get to lay claim to my vehicle?"

"See. I knew you were a fast learner." I tapped her on her temple and went back to my eggs. Our friendship had progressed quickly in the random moments our paths crossed during the day. In the hall outside our rooms. On the beach as she headed off to work her magic on a client. In the kitchen as we made meals. I'd learned her schedule and planned my path so we'd be most likely to meet. If I was honest, that was the reason I hurried through getting ready today, so I wouldn't miss her before she got busy.

Cat rolled her eyes. "What makes you think you even know how to handle my Jeep?"

I put my fork down and stared at her, incredulous. Pink flared across her cheekbones, highlighting her eyes. I loved it when she blushed. It made her even more beautiful. "Oh gee," I said, scrunching up my face. "Let me see. It couldn't be all the time I've spent in Humvees and Growlers. On second thought, your Jeep is definitely more than I can handle. I'm glad you mentioned it."

Cat gave me an exasperated look. "I think I might like it more when you're all intense and glowery. At least then you're not busy being a dick."

"Such language," I said, smiling wickedly as I shoved another bite of eggs in my mouth. She made a face and went back to her phone. I watched her for a few minutes before she finally turned back to me.

"Fine." She sighed deeply. "I *suppose* I can let you drive the Jeep."

"Oh no." I held up my hands. "Don't do me any favors."

She slapped me on the arm, an adorable smile playing across her face. "You're terrible." She turned to Caleb. "Is he always like this?"

Caleb grunted. "He's going easy on you." He dropped her a wink and she laughed before turning her attention back to me.

"I'll be done with my last client around six. I'll give you the keys to the Jeep, but you have to promise to take me somewhere delicious to eat. Take it or leave it, Hutton."

"Oh, I'll take it," I said as Cat gathered her bowl and stood. She gave me a mock salute on her way out of the kitchen. Harlow shook her head as she strummed and Caleb laughed into his plate.

"What?" I asked.

"You two are something else," Harlow replied while Caleb vigorously nodded his agreement.

"What's that supposed to mean?"

"It means why don't you flirt a little harder next time?"

"Whatever. We're not flirting. She's just easy to talk to."

"Whatever you need to tell yourself."

"I don't need to tell myself anything. Facts are facts, little sister."

Harlow made a face that meant she believed me not at all and I excused myself from the table.

Being with Cat was easy. Ever since that night on our balconies, it felt like she'd been part of my life for years and not weeks. Her quick humor and sharp mind kept me on my toes. I respected her work ethic and her desire to be better today than she was the day before. I looked forward to seeing her and then spent the whole time checking my phone for an email from Katydid. I felt drawn to them both, attracted to them both, and very, very confused. I needed to believe Cat and I weren't flirting. That we were just friends. Otherwise, what I was doing was wrong.

While part of me screamed that Katydid had shown up in my life first, the other part countered that Cat was here now, in the flesh. Even though I had never met Katydid, I knew her in ways I had never known another person, and she had parts of me I thought I would always keep for myself. Cat was wonderful and she was fun and she was *real*, but my loyalty belonged to a woman I'd not yet met.

CHAPTER TWENTY-THREE

CAT

I sunk my teeth into a giant burger and smiled around the bite, grease trickling down my fingers as I chewed. "Delicious," I said, my voice muffled by food, not caring even a little bit about manners or being polite. A sandwich this good needed recognized and I knew Lucas wouldn't mind. He liked me even if I did have too much burger in my mouth.

"So, I was right?" Lucas swirled a fry through a mound of ketchup and popped it into his mouth.

"Of course you were right. When aren't you right?"

We sat on a picnic bench outside a little hole in the wall burger joint right on the edge of the water. With rickety wood and a hand-painted sign, the place looked more like a shack than a restaurant. To say I'd been dubious when we pulled into the crowded parking lot would be an understatement. When I voiced my reservations, he told me that if a place this dingy could attract such a large crowd, then the food had to be amazing. And it was. Oh man, it was.

Lucas sat across from me, as relaxed as I'd ever seen him. We were both sweaty and windblown from a long evening in the Jeep and thoroughly infatuated with our adventure...

...with the food...

...with each other...

He cocked his head and grimaced. "I wasn't right when I thought I was taking us to a great place to go off-roading and it turned out to be a golf course."

"This is true." I swiped my napkin across my hands, then wrestled another handful out of the metal container on the table. "For a guy who commandeered my Jeep with the promise of showing me around, it sure seems like you've been figuring this whole evening out on the fly." I scooped my burger off my plate and took another bite. Lucas shook his head as grease slid across my newly cleaned fingers.

"I *was* figuring it out on the fly." He narrowed his eyes. "Remember the part where I told you I'd been gone awhile? You know, left town as soon as I could to get away from an ever more abusive dad, joined the

Marines, and then died in Afghanistan? Hence, the perfect place to go off-roading is now a golf course...?"

His eyes tightened with his Afghanistan statement, but I pretended not to notice. He hadn't spoken about that day since he told me about it on the boat. The fact that he mentioned it now seemed like progress. "Of course I remember. But I also remember you telling me you would 'show me around.'" I lowered my burger to my plate and made air quotes, then slurped at my soda. "How did you ever think you would accomplish that when you didn't know where you were going either?"

"Well, I showed you the golf course, didn't I? And I believe it was my fantastic navigation skills that led us to discover this here burger joint."

"Whatever, Lucas." I met his gaze across the table and widened my eyes. "Being lost doesn't count," I joked.

Lucas studied me, the levity slipping from his face. "We're all lost, babe. All of us. If anyone tries to make you believe he knows what he's doing, he's full of shit. Every day is nothing more than trying to find your way forward. The trick is figuring out how to turn the confusion into a good time, otherwise life is going to suck."

The man had a point. Even when my life was on the right track and moving in the right direction, I had no clue what I was doing. Looking back, I'd fallen out of love with Nash a long time ago, and he'd fallen out of love with me years before that. As much as I told myself my job at Utopia had been so I could start working as a masseuse without having to figure out how to run a business at the same time, a part of me wondered if Nash had been right after all. Maybe I had been stalling...

"For the record," Lucas continued, "I completely disagree with your word choice. We weren't lost. We were *discovering*. It's all in how you sell it, Cat. Christopher Columbus was lost as hell, but he knew how to spin it and now the man has a national holiday."

"He knew how to spin it?" The image of Christopher Columbus spinning his accidental discovery to the king and queen of Spain made me chuckle.

"Anyway, are you really going to tell me you didn't have fun tonight?" Lucas lifted an eyebrow, daring me to be honest.

I pursed my lips, as if I was weighing options. The truth was, I had a blast. We took the roof and doors off the Jeep and drove until we got lost, then drove some more until we found something interesting. I sang loudly to whatever came on the radio while my hair whipped in the wind. Every time I looked at Lucas, I caught him already staring at me and I loved what I thought I saw in his eyes. We were wild and free, but I felt completely safe, like no matter how many wrong turns we took, we'd end up exactly where we were supposed to be.

"See?" Lucas pointed a fry my way. "That's what I thought."

I dropped my jaw. "I didn't even say anything."

"You didn't have to. The look on your face said it all."

"Uh-huh. And now you're a mind reader?"

"I am. It's one of the many surprising and wonderful things you've yet to discover about me."

I pushed my plate away and folded my arms on the table. "I see."

"You don't yet," Lucas said with a look that made my knees weak. "But you will."

The night was hot and humid and sweat trailed down my back. The hair at my temples curled and I watched as Lucas came to life in front of me, stepping out from behind the troubled Marine and showing me the man he was inside. We talked about whatever came to mind, teasing and laughing during the silly stuff and leaning in close and lowering our voices during the serious parts.

Once again, our conversation wandered around that day in Afghanistan. He explained not one, but two bombs that nearly ended his life and then fell silent. I watched him battle the memories, then visibly shake them off. He skipped the rest of the details, and continued his story after he woke up at Landstuhl Medical Center in Germany. He told me that Harlow couldn't bring herself to visit him in the hospital once he made it back to the States because of their dad.

I shook my head. "That says everything about your father," I said. "It had to kill her not to be there for you." Lucas looked uncertain and I hurried on. "I know it probably didn't feel all that great on your end either, but the fact that Harlow couldn't bring herself to face your dad in order to be there when you needed her? I mean, that speaks volumes. The five of you would do anything for each other."

All the light bled from Lucas' face. "Anything except come see me the day I died."

His words were hollow. They hit me hard and I sat back, stunned by what I saw in his eyes. Silence invaded the space between us and I felt like a stranger. Like I'd crossed some invisible boundary and spoken when I should have stayed silent. I thought we'd come past that. I thought we had gotten to a place where we could start being honest with each other. Apparently, I was wrong.

The last two weeks at the Hut had been just as wonderful as they were confusing. While the Huttons had welcomed me with open arms, making me feel like part of the family, my friendship with Lucas had deepened. While his mood still darkened now and again, the more time we spent together, the more he let the light shine through his scars. If I had my way, I'd never see the darker side of him again. I wanted to be the light that chased away his demons.

We talked and we talked and we talked, and while he opened up about his past, I stayed close-lipped about mine. It wasn't purposeful. I wanted to be as open with him as he was with me, but every time I started to talk about Nash, about the years we spent together, about the day I came home to find him giving the attention I so desperately needed to another woman, I found myself changing the topic.

The way Lucas looked at me made me feel like I was coming to life and the possibility that knowing my past would change the way he saw me kept my lips tightly sealed. I was afraid that if he knew I wasn't enough for Nash, he would realize I was too flawed to love.

I shared stories about my mom. Talked about my dad. Laughed over those awkward years in middle school, but whenever we got to recent history, I changed the topic to him.

Meanwhile, Skywalker poked and prodded, learning all the things that had shaped and defined me, all the things I couldn't give Lucas. Skywalker got my deepest thoughts, my hopes and fears, and Lucas got the rest of me.

There were times I wondered if what I was doing with the two of them was wrong, if somehow, I was being disloyal. The more our relationships deepened, the more I questioned. But since Skywalker was little more than an email address, and Lucas was little more than a friend, I couldn't see how staying in both their lives was a bad thing.

Except everything about that statement was a lie.

There was a man behind Skywalker's email address. A man with deep thoughts and a big heart. A man who spoke to me like I mattered. A man who took the worst of me and came back calling me beautiful. A man I could easily fall in love with.

And, sitting here across from Lucas, my stomach twisting and turning, my heart tightening every time he smiled, I knew he was so much more than a friend. I could easily fall in love with him, too. Guilt settled onto my shoulders and I put my burger down, suddenly not at all hungry.

"What's wrong?" Lucas asked, folding his arms on the table and leaning forward.

I smiled. "Not a damn thing."

"Liar."

I cocked an eyebrow. "Liar? Really?"

"Yep. I'm psychic, remember?" He laughed, but I could tell by the way his eyes searched mine that he was very aware something wasn't right.

"I remember you're full of shit." I sucked on my straw but got nothing more than a slurp of watered-down soda. "I just got caught in deep thoughts. I really like hanging out with you."

"And that's a deep thought?"

"Actually, it is." I was treading on thin ice, walking dangerously close to a topic I wasn't ready to talk about.

Lucas scooped up another fry. "I like hanging out with you, too" he said, and something in the way he looked at me said it was a deep thought for him, too.

CHAPTER TWENTY-FOUR

CAT

I woke to Lucas muttering and moaning on the other side of the wall. As my eyes fluttered open, his sounds set off a carnal flare in my belly. I pressed my ear to the wall, listening hard. Was Lucas pleasuring himself?

A sense of voyeuristic delight flooded my system as I listened, imagining each illicit act that might warrant what I heard. But, as the cobwebs of sleep cleared from my mind, I realized that I wasn't hearing Lucas engaged in some sexy moment of abandon.

I was listening to one of his nightmares.

Twice before, I'd been woken by him talking in his sleep, his fear evident even though it was muffled by the wall. My initial urge had been to go to him, to wake him and to comfort him. The last time, I made it into the hallway before I realized how epically presumptuous I was being. I had crawled back into bed, imagining all my positive thoughts as a golden field, streaming through the wall between us. It felt a little silly, but I needed to do something and that had been the only thing I could come up with.

Tonight though, as his murmured exclamations grew more and more frantic, I couldn't stop myself. I flung back my covers, padded into the hallway, and carefully knocked on his door. "Lucas?" I whispered, aware of the sleeping Hutton siblings and the obviously thin walls on the third floor.

When nothing happened, I knocked again. The sounds of his nightmare faded and I realized that I was standing in the hallway, wearing nothing but a thin tank top and teeny shorts, checking on a man who probably had more skills than I did at chasing away the demons he fought.

I was just about to give up and head back to my room when Lucas cracked open the door. "Cat?" His voice was harsh and raw. He leaned on the doorjamb, shirtless, disheveled, and sexy as hell.

"I'm sorry," I whispered. "You just sounded so..." I shrugged. "Your nightmare...it sounded like a bad one. I wanted to make sure you're okay."

I suddenly felt ridiculous. What comfort could I

offer this man when I barely knew him? When he had shut down so completely when I asked him about his scars?

Lucas dropped his gaze to his feet, his brow furrowing. After a few silent seconds, he met my eyes and scowled. "They're all bad. But that was one of the worst."

He didn't say anything else and I started to retreat, whispering a slew of excuses. Lucas swung his door the rest of the way open, stopping me in my tracks. "Come outside with me?"

Though the request was odd, I didn't hesitate. I didn't take into consideration that it was the middle of the night. Or that I was wearing very little clothing. I didn't take into consideration his bare chest or our bare feet. I simply nodded and followed him downstairs. On the way, he swiped a set of keys off the counter, then led me through the kitchen and out the back door. Lucas took my hand as we trudged through the sand, leading me toward the dock.

"Where are we going?" I asked.

"You're not afraid of being on the water in the dark, are you? I just...sometimes...I just need to submerge myself in something bigger than I am." He turned a wounded gaze my way as we came to a stop in front of the boat. "Come with me?"

The twin flames lit by my accidental fantasies

about him the other night combined with what I thought I heard when I first woke up. My body surged with desire for him and threatened to burn me alive. I nodded without speaking and took Lucas' outstretched hand. The contact did very little to douse the lust throbbing in my lower belly.

He guided me through helping him get the boat untied from the dock, then wordlessly navigated us out to sea. When we were surrounded by nothing but water and sky, he killed the engine. The ocean lapped against the boat as we rocked, aimless and at the mercy of the waves. The moon hung low and swollen over the water, its reflection rippling and undulating ahead of us.

I tipped my head back as a breeze caused me to shiver. "Oh, Lucas! Look at all the stars." Goosebumps rippled down my bare arms and I wasn't sure if it was the view, the chill in the air...or the man.

"They're the only thing that ever makes me feel better. The stars and the sea." He shrugged, almost embarrassed by the admission. "Cold?"

I nodded.

"Come here." His voice was gruff, almost ashamed, as he beckoned me toward him. He rubbed his hands along my arms, his bare skin warm and lush against mine. "You have to see this," he whispered, then stretched out on the bottom of the boat, holding out an arm, inviting me to curl in next to him.

I did, overly aware of the long line of contact between us. Our bodies fit together so nicely, my curves against his angles. Hard meeting soft. My mind turned treacherous, offering me images of all the hardest parts on Lucas' body. I distracted myself by following his gaze up to the sky and forgot everything. "I have no words," I murmured, lost in the beauty of the heavens stretched above. It was as if I could see the entire universe, presented as a gift for us and us alone.

Lucas grunted an affirmation. "Sometimes it's the only thing that makes me feel better," he said. "Knowing that throughout all our history, all the ups and downs of human existence, the stars will always burn. The moon will always glow. The sky is endless."

I nuzzled closer. His sentiment echoed my mother's so closely, it brought me an odd sense of comfort. And in that comfort, I grew bold. "What do you dream about?" I asked, then wished I could shove my words right back into my mouth.

I waited for him to tense. To push me away. To close up and withdraw like he did the last time we were in this boat, when I asked about his scars.

He didn't do any of those things. In fact, it almost felt like he pulled me closer, though it was quite possible I imagined that last bit.

Lucas let out a long sigh. "Mostly, I dream about that night."

He didn't need to elaborate. I knew he was talking about what happened in Afghanistan. I grew still, breathing in the scent of his skin, while the boat rocked in the waves and the stars glittered in the black velvet sky.

"The first blast sent me flying out of the way of the second, so in that I was lucky. But my commanding officer, Captain Reed, wasn't so lucky. The second blast was worse, and as he came running toward me, to make sure I was okay, he got hit. I watched it happen." Lucas paused and I got the sense he was struggling to find the right words. When he finally spoke, his voice was thick. "And I dream of that over and over. Every night, reliving every single detail."

"I'm sorry that happened to you."

"I am too."

"Did he live?" I asked. "Captain Reed?"

"He did. Has a family somewhere in Ohio, I think. Probably what helped him recover so quickly. Knowing he had people relying on him. Waiting on him."

"What helped you recover? Your family?"

Lucas laughed. "I'm a stubborn son of a bitch. I couldn't give in. Even when it felt like the easiest thing was to close my eyes and never open them again, I just couldn't do that. Couldn't give those assholes the satisfaction. They wanted me dead? Well, I'm very much alive."

I pushed up on an elbow and stared down at him. My hair tumbled over a shoulder, cascading around us. His gaze settled on mine and then flickered across my face. Across my lips. My throat. My jawline. He took in my details and I felt like he was committing me to memory.

"The moon makes it look like you're wearing a halo," he said. "Like you're an angel, come down to take care of me."

I wanted to take care of him. I wanted to bandage up the scars across his psyche, the wounds slashed on his heart and soul, and bring him strength and joy. I wanted to make him smile. I wanted to chase away the nightmares.

And, more than anything, I very much wanted to kiss him. I couldn't draw my eyes away from his lips, from the soft smattering of stubble along his jawline. I wanted his arms around me and his taste on my tongue. I wanted to devour his terror and bring him peace.

Instead, I smiled and lay down next to him, careful to keep some distance between us.

"Thank you for coming to check on me," he murmured.

"Thank you for bringing me out here," I replied. We lay quietly for some time, watching the stars and feeling the roll of the ocean. When Lucas suggested it was time to get back, I didn't know if I was relieved or disappointed.

What I did know was that I was very, very confused.

CHAPTER TWENTY-FIVE

FROM: KATYDID <GETOVERYOURSELF@IMAIL.COM>
to: Skywalker
<themanwhofoundyourjournal@imail.com>
date: September 2, 2018 at 8:02 pm
subject: WASSUP!!!

Hey you! How's your day been? Mine has been great. Life is settling into a rhythm. It's been what? Almost a month and a half since I left Nash? I'm starting to feel comfortable in my new normal.

Okay...

You know what?

That's a load of bull.

Yes, I'm comfortable. And YES, I'm happy. Happier than I think I've ever been. Or at least I should be. It's just, something's been bothering me and no matter how hard I try to tell myself it doesn't mean anything, I can't get it out of my head.

Do you think the fact that Nash cheated on me means there's something wrong with me? Do you think it means I'm broken? Flawed? If you met me in person and we were chatting and then you found out that I left my fiancé because I caught him in bed with another woman, after what? MONTHS of not having a physical connection worth a damn? Would you wonder what in the world was wrong with me that would make a man like Nash want someone else?

I know what you're going to say. Nash is a fool who couldn't see what was in front of him.

But he's also a good man. Hard-working. Successful. He had my dad's seal of approval and while my dad draws hard lines, those hard lines make his approval mean something.

So, what is wrong with me that would make Nash care so *little* that he would do what he did? If he cared at all, he would have tried to fight for us. But our relationship, one that we'd been in since high school, it wasn't worth fighting for in his eyes. He'd rather bring another woman home, to my bed, to get what he needed. He didn't care...

What's that say about me?

Have you ever been cheated on? It's a betrayal of

trust in the worst degree. It makes me look back on the years Nash and I spent together and second guess all of it. Were the good times as good as I remember? Or was he cheating on me then, too? Did he really keep putting off the wedding because he was busy? Or did he honestly not want to get married?

None of this matters.

That part of my life is over.

I know I need to get past it.

And it's not like I miss him, I just have this huge hole of self-doubt in my chest and I don't know what to do about it.

I hit send and collapsed back on my bed to stare at the whirls and swirls patterned into the ceiling. I fidgeted with the hem of my shirt. Shifted positions. Stood and checked my reflection, smoothing a hair I couldn't see away from my eyes. I paced, anxiety buzzing in my veins, gnawing at my thoughts, digging its fingers into my heart. I couldn't understand my reaction until realization stopped me in my tracks.

Here I was, lamenting the challenges of being cheated on, while carrying on a relationship with two men. I sank to the edge of my bed, my jaw slack. Lucas and I were just friends, and yet we weren't. I knew what 'just friends' felt like and whatever it was that happened between us when we got together was so much more.

We'd never touched. Never kissed. Never talked about any kind of feelings for each other, but they were there. At least for me. The way his voice made my stomach clench, his laugh warmed my heart. I thought about him when we weren't together and as I lay in bed at night, I was overly aware of him just a few feet away, the two of us separated by nothing more than an incredibly thin wall.

And then there was Skywalker. And damn it! I didn't even know his name! But I gave him parts of myself that I kept from Lucas—more than I'd ever given another person. And I gave Lucas parts of myself that I kept from Skywalker.

I wasn't with either of them, but I wasn't separate from them either. What would I do if Lucas asked for more? If he had tried to kiss me the other night on the boat? The thought of his lips on mine made my head spin and my core tighten. Imagining his hands in my hair, the scrape of his stubble against my lips, his rough touch sliding up my back awakened feelings in me I hadn't experienced in so long I'd forgotten what they were.

What would I do if Skywalker gave me his name? If he asked to meet at the coffee shop in Galveston? I'd love to stare that man in the face, to let his real name roll off my tongue. I'd love to thank him for all the support he had given me, all the beautiful words he'd sent my way.

And I just asked him if I was flawed because Nash cheated on me. It felt more like I was flawed because I was willing to cheat. Except, did this count as cheating? Really? I wasn't actually involved with either man, although I'd be devastated to lose either one.

For all the talk about wearing masks, I realized I'd been hiding from myself as well. I wasn't the kind of person I thought I was. Confusion weighed heavily on me, but I was up and moving again, unable to sit still with all the thoughts spinning around and around inside.

When my phone pinged with a response, I almost didn't read it. I didn't want to see what kindness Skywalker had for me when I'd taken him for granted. I was taking without giving in return. The worst kind of fool.

Lucas' sliding glass door hissed open and suddenly I needed fresh air more than anything. I needed to fling open my own door and step out onto the balcony and soak up all the attention he could give me because when Lucas looked at me, he saw the person I wanted to be, not the person I was. I wanted to bask in the way

his eyes settled on mine and ignore this rattle in the pit
of my stomach.

But I didn't go outside.

I opened Skywalker's email.

———————

from: Skywalker
<themanwhofoundyourjournal@imail.com>
    to: Katydid <getoveryourself@imail.com>
    date: September 2, 2018 at 8:10 pm
    subject: RE: WASSUP!!!

YOU. ARE. NOT. FLAWED.

———————

from: Katydid <getoveryourself@imail.com>
    to: Skywalker
<themanwhofoundyourjournal@imail.com>
    date: September 2, 2018 at 8:11 pm
    subject: sigh

Oh, but I am.

from: Skywalker
<themanwhofoundyourjournal@imail.com>
    to: Katydid <getoveryourself@imail.com>
    date: September 2, 2018 at 8:20 pm
    subject: sighing back

Okay, fine. You're flawed. So am I. So is everyone else.
You're human, Katydid. No one is perfect, but you're
pretty damn close.

from: Katydid <getoveryourself@imail.com>
    to: Skywalker
<themanwhofoundyourjournal@imail.com>
    date: September 2, 2018 at 8:20 pm
    subject: RE: sighing back

Says the man who's never actually met me...

I waited for a response. Phone in hand. Staring at a

black screen. Breath held. Shoulders tense. I gave him the perfect set up to ask me out.

And if he asked me to meet him, I would. Right or wrong, I'd head back to Galveston for the weekend and I'd finally meet this man face to face. I could hug him and thank him and see if he was as amazing in person as he was via email. Seconds turned into minutes and confidence faded into indecision.

I dropped my phone on my bed and slid open my balcony door to find Lucas sitting, elbows on knees, head in his hands. He glanced up when I stepped out and the look in his eyes nearly stopped my heart.

"Hey," I said, sliding my door closed.

"Hey."

"Bad night?" I leaned on the railing separating us.

He shrugged. Looked like he was going to say something, then swallowed his words. "I'm sorry, Cat," he said as he stood. "I can't tonight." He slid open his door, turned and when his eyes hit mine the sadness I saw shattered my heart. Without another word, he shut the door, closed the blinds, and left me alone with my thoughts.

CHAPTER TWENTY-SIX

Cat

The next morning, I woke before anyone else in the house was moving. Outside my window, threads of pink and purple streaked up from the horizon. I watched with disinterest as my thoughts buzzed, a swarm of gnats flicking through my awareness. After Lucas left me outside, I spent a long night awake and alone with my thoughts. I wasn't the kind of woman who focused on the bad stuff, nor was I the kind of woman who used people or led them on. I had the creeping feeling I was doing a little of both right now.

I got dressed and brushed my teeth, took a moment in the mirror to run a brush through my hair and then stared into the eyes reflected back at me. I saw my mother in their shape and my father in their color and wondered where that left me. My whole life, I'd considered myself stuck somewhere between them, a culmination of their totally opposite personalities. Maybe it was time to think of myself as simply *me*. I was who I was, despite my upbringing, despite my parents, despite everything.

With thoughts that big swimming through my head, I needed outside where I could stare at things bigger and older than me and put my life into perspective. I crept through the quiet house and gently pulled the door shut behind me, feeling marginally better the moment I took a long breath of fresh air. I climbed into my Jeep, humming a wordless little tune, and drove straight to my mom's. I needed to talk with someone who wouldn't judge me, and my mother would love me no matter how bad my choices had been lately.

My Jeep crawled over the dirt road leading to her little plot of land and I found her already outside, sipping at a cup of coffee. She turned as I killed the engine and smiled when she saw me, though she looked tired and it took her longer than usual to push herself out of her chair. I wrapped my arms around her, and it felt like there was less of her. Her body, her energy, everything was small and tight.

"To what do I owe this wonderful gift on a Saturday morning?" she asked as she ran a hand through my hair, then stepped out of my hug. She waved me over and I grabbed my chair from its place near the RV and set it up beside hers.

"I needed my mom."

She turned to me with watchful eyes, her momma-bear claws already out. "What's wrong, Katydid?"

Maybe it was the look. Maybe it was hearing that nickname, the one only she and Skywalker used. Maybe it was sitting outside under the sky, staring at the water, feeling the unmatched love of a mother for her daughter.

I broke.

I poured out everything I'd kept bottled up over the last six weeks. Mom listened while I purged my soul of secrets. My friendship with Lucas, the emails back and forth with a stranger, and the budding feelings I had for both of them.

"But I haven't even met Skywalker," I said, running my hands into my hair. "And he hasn't asked for more than my nickname, so maybe we don't mean that much to each other after all? I go round and round, wondering if I'm being too hard on myself at the same time I feel awful for being a hypocrite. I mean, I'm complaining about cheating when I'm not exactly being faithful." Once it was all out in the open, I laughed because what else could I do?

"Oh, sweet Cat." Mom placed a hand on mine. "I

can think of far worse problems than having two men to fall in love with."

I was well aware that in the scheme of things, my problem was far from earth-shattering, and proceeded to say as much.

Mom waved my statement away. "I'm not trying to diminish your feelings. You're caught. You're confused. I understand. Here's my advice, and it's fantastic as usual. If things are to go any farther with either of these men, you need to pick one and let the other fall to the wayside. But, dear, sweet daughter, life is too fragile to waste time feeling this bad about a thing that hasn't happened yet. You're not involved with either man. Make a choice before you are." She smiled, pleased with the simplicity of her advice, while her statement caught my attention and ran away with it.

Life is too fragile...

The thought had me off-guard, my subconscious connecting dots I hadn't made sense of yet, but I shook my head and refocused on our conversation. "So, what should I do?" I asked. "Who should I pick?"

Mom sighed and her features softened. "I can't tell you what to do, Katydid. You're the only one who knows the answer to that question." It was such a typical answer from her, I should have known better than to ask in the first place.

I studied her, the familiar lines of her face bringing

me some measure of peace. There's nothing quite as comforting as knowing, without a doubt, that you are loved. "Fine, what would *you* do?"

"I would spend my energy on the sure thing." Mom nodded with conviction.

"So...Lucas?"

Mom eyed me. "Is he the sure thing?"

Was Lucas the sure thing? His name was the first that came to mind, but the moment I spoke, I wondered about my mystery man.

"He's the one I see every day."

"You went years without seeing me and that didn't affect us one little bit." Again, her statement caught my attention. More dots were connected and still, I couldn't make sense of what my subconscious had already figured out.

"Yeah, but you're my mom. We'll always be good, you know?"

She bit the inside of her lip and looked at me so strangely, my breath caught in my chest.

"Hey Mom?" I started, not sure what I was going to ask until the words left me lips. "Are you okay?"

I expected her to brush off my worry. To smile and tell me she was more than okay, she was fabulous. That's what Mom did. She woke each morning with a smile on her face and gratitude falling from her lips. She called challenges 'learning experiences' and sent

God a silent thank you for every obstacle he set in her path because getting up when you fall down only made you stronger.

Instead, her face fell. "You know what, Catherine? I'm not okay." I couldn't remember the last time she used my full name. The hairs on the back of my neck and arms stood on end. My blood froze in my veins. My stomach dropped to my feet.

"What's wrong, Mom?" I asked, even though that still-small voice was screaming the answer in my head.

"I'm sick." She shifted in her seat and gave her focus to the ocean. Her face went slack and her skin looked gray and sallow in the morning light. Her hair was thin and colorless.

"How sick?"

"Very sick." She turned to me, sadness softening her gaze. "I have cancer."

The words were a whisper, but I wanted to cover my ears against the sound.

"How bad?" I asked, though I already knew. If we were talking about it, it was bad.

"That's the thing. I've *had* cancer. It's the reason I bought this damn RV in the first place."

She explained about the diagnosis that came the year I turned twelve. Doctors throwing around words like 'terminal' as if they weren't talking about her life, about our life, about *my* life. She hadn't been able to make peace with telling me. The thought of me having to watch her grow sick and whither and die just as my own life was supposed to be starting sickened her. And so, instead of making me live through her death, she decided to take off. See the country. Spend her last years doing the things she wanted, sending me postcards with happy thoughts and hiding her tragedy behind phone calls so I couldn't see the illness etched into her face.

Mom smiled sadly. "I didn't want their poison in my veins, making my last years miserable. I wanted to go off and die with dignity. Funny thing. Instead of getting sicker, I got better."

Her words pushed into my head and banged against the inside of my skull. They made an awful kind of sense, but I couldn't wrap my mind around her story. "Didn't you think it would have been easier for me to handle your death if I'd had time to get right with it? Instead of it coming as a surprise and ripping the rug right out from underneath me?"

"Believe me, I agonized over what was right. But I wanted you to remember me as I was, not as an invalid..." She choked on the rest of the sentence and trailed off. My mind followed hers, out of the past and into the present, then...the future.

"It's back?" I asked and the answer was written all

over her body, the dots my subconscious mind connected the first time I saw her six weeks ago.

She nodded. "And there's no running away from it this time. I don't expect God doles out more than one miracle per lifetime."

"Oh, Mom." I stood, only to drop to my knees in front of her. "I'm so sorry. I'm here. You're not alone." I offered a million platitudes and asked as many questions as I could, trying to understand everything all at once. Her answers led to more questions and we talked all morning. I added her doctor's appointments into my calendar and made the decision to move out of The Hut. I'd sleep on a damn table for the rest of my life if it meant my mom wouldn't have to go through this alone.

I'd explain to the Huttons on Monday, but the rest of this weekend belonged to my mom.

CHAPTER TWENTY-SEVEN

Lucas

God, I was such an asshole. When we first met, I swore to Katydid that she was special, that any man who would take without giving was a fool. Yet here I was, slowly falling for Cat, while Katydid gave me her soul.

Her last email challenged me to ask her to meet, and I couldn't rise to the challenge. Still reeling from her email about cheating, I couldn't even find the strength to respond and tell her I was in Florida. I shut down my phone and went dark. Just another jerk who turned his back on her.

And the moment I saw Cat on the balcony, I ran away from her, too.

Sleep was a pipedream, so I stole down the stairs,

unsure as to what I would do once I got there, and found Harlow at the kitchen table, fingers flying over the keys of her laptop. Her long blonde hair blocked her face from view, but I knew her brows were scrunched up, her tongue caught between her teeth. It was her writing face, the one she wore when the words were flowing freely and she existed more in her story world than this one. Not wanting to interrupt her, I froze in the doorway.

"It's okay, Luc" my sister said from behind her wall of hair. "You're not bothering me."

"How'd you know it was me?" I crossed the kitchen, pulled out a chair, and sat.

Harlow finished typing, then closed her laptop and flipped her hair over her shoulder. "You limp."

My jaw dropped and I let out a short cough of a laugh. "I do not." And I was damn proud of the fact. I worked hard to keep my gait natural and even. Sometimes it took constant conscious effort to keep the pain out of my face and my steps rhythmic, but I put in the effort. Every day, I fought my body.

Harlow rested her elbow on the table and her cheek in her hand. "You do. It's small. You fool everyone else, but you can't fool me." She shrugged and opened her laptop, eyes scanning the screen. "I don't know why you fight your scars. They're part of what makes you interesting."

"Remind me not to sit down with you while you're writing ever again. You're looking for depth that isn't here."

"Oh, come on. It's the stories we have to tell that makes life worth living. I dare you tell me a story worth hearing that doesn't leave a scar or two and I'll stop trying to get published this instant and get a job as a waitress."

I exhaled deeply and leaned my head against the back of my chair. "I don't want to argue with you." I didn't have it in me. I came downstairs for peace, for a chance to clear my head. The last thing I needed was for Harlow to fill it back up again with something new to worry about.

"Who said we're arguing? I just think you should stop trying to hide all the parts that make you worth knowing and you're busy trying to prove to me that you're perfectly normal." She pounded on the backspace button a few times then glanced at me. "Perfect is boring, by the way."

"And how, pray tell, is what you just described *not* arguing?"

"It's called having a discussion, dumbass. You should try it sometime. Or did all those years of blatantly following orders without having to think for yourself erase that part of you, too?"

I sat forward. "Excuse me?"

"Hey. Sorry." She closed her laptop and held up her hands. "I crossed a line. You're right. I'm too far into my story right now and am looking for mind-blowing epiphanies where they don't belong. You know I respect the hell out of your Marine ass."

"You mean my bionic ass." I smirked.

Harlow smiled. "Whatever." She knew I could never be mad at her for long. As the oldest, I always stood up for my younger sister, even against myself. Her honesty, while sometimes annoying, was refreshing. "Now," she began with concern in her eyes, "what has you wandering this late while the rest of the house is sleeping?"

I almost shrugged off her question, but since I was in the market for a mind-blowing epiphany and she seemed in the perfect mood to give one, I told her everything. I opened my heart and bled for her, talking without thinking, chasing down thoughts only to find they led to more questions. I explained Katydid and Cat. I told her about the nightmares I was still having. I told her I had no idea where I was going and wondered how in the world I could keep moving forward when it was like navigating a thick jungle. Alone. No path. No guide.

Harlow listened to it all and when I ran out of words she smiled. "How do you keep moving forward? The answer is simple. You limp."

I rolled my eyes. "Harlow..."

"I'm being serious here. When you got to the hospital in Germany, the doctors told us you probably wouldn't survive the night. But you did. Then, when they decided to send you back to the States, they told us there was a chance you might not survive the flight. But you did. And then they told us you might never walk again..." She raised an eyebrow.

"But I did."

"And it sucked at first, didn't it?"

I nodded.

"And it hurt and you hated it and you wanted to stop but you kept going. And at first, your limp was so pronounced, you looked like an old man, hobbling down the hallway. But you kept going and it kept getting better and now you barely limp at all."

"I don't limp."

"You do. But if you keep fighting the way you do, I'm sure that limp will go away completely."

I stared at her with narrowed eyes. Somewhere in there, my sister had a point, but I couldn't find it for the life of me. "You lost me, Harlow..."

"What I'm saying is that you can't ignore your problems. You can't whitewash them away, saying you don't limp when you do, ignoring your scars and expecting the rest of us to ignore them, too. But you can fight through them enough to see what's on the other side. You keep walking long enough, you're going to get somewhere."

"How is any of this supposed to help me with Cat and Katydid?"

"Explain the problem to me again."

"I met Katydid's soul and she's the most beautiful person I've ever known, but I don't *know* anything about her. And Cat? I can't think straight when I'm around her. Hours pass and they feel like minutes and we talk and we laugh, but she's holding her soul back from me. She's keeping part of herself separate and I need all of her. Besides, I met Katydid first. I can't be another man who takes from her without giving in return. I can't be someone else who stares at all of her and then walks right into another woman's arms. I can't be that man."

"Then don't be that man. Get your ass to Galveston and find your mystery woman."

"But what about Cat?"

"You can't live in between decisions, big brother. Sooner or later, it'll all come crumbling down and you'll get caught in the wreckage." Harlow smiled. "Now, go away because I need to write all of that down so I can use it later."

She smirked but didn't say anything else. I stood as her fingers flew over keys.

"At least promise you won't kill me off this time?"

"Can't promise anything," she said, shooing me off without looking up.

The next day I woke early and got my run, analyzing my gait for the limp Harlow swore she saw while I let our conversation replay through my head. While I didn't find the limp, I did discover her point. I had to make good on my promise to Katydid before I could do anything with Cat. I went upstairs, showered, and then knocked on Cat's door.

I wanted to apologize for walking away from her last night on the balcony, for leading her on when I was already partially involved with someone else. I wanted to explain everything. She deserved it, even though I knew things wouldn't go well.

At best, she'd be confused.

At worst, she'd be mad.

But at least she'd have the truth.

But Cat never answered her door and when I walked downstairs and looked outside, her Jeep wasn't in the parking lot. She was gone and she rarely left without letting me know her plans.

Something was wrong. I could feel it. I headed off in search of something to occupy my time, worrying and worrying and worrying.

CHAPTER TWENTY-EIGHT

Cat

My mom had decades to come to terms with her diagnosis, but I needed more than a day and a half to make peace with her mortality. I spent the rest of the weekend with her, fluttering around like a nervous hen, as if I could cure her cancer by keeping her quiet and cared for. I brought her drinks. Cooked the meals. Did the dishes. Tucked her into bed. And was waiting with fresh coffee the minute she opened her eyes in the morning, all the while wondering if the caffeine would be more helpful or harmful. By the time I had to leave for work on Monday morning, I imagined she was almost glad for a bit of quiet sanity.

I arrived at the Hut with just enough time to

shower and change my clothes before I had to meet my first client. The rush of hot water beat at my shoulders, matting my hair to my back. Tears pricked at my eyes, but I brushed them away. To give in to the tears would open the floodgates of anger, betrayal, bitterness, and loss—and I didn't have time to indulge my emotions right now. I needed to keep going. For my clients. For my mom. For me.

I turned the knob on the faucet, making the water so cold it felt like needles pricking my skin. The only thing I could focus on was getting clean as fast as I could and all I could feel was cold, cold, cold. The frigid water obliterated the worry and the fear. For a moment, anyway. As soon as I stepped out of the shower, shivering as I toweled off, it all came rushing back.

Saturday night, after a slew of concerned texts from Lucas, I finally responded, explaining that I'd be gone all weekend. Told him I was spending the time with my mom, but avoided the details. He seemed to sense there was something I wasn't saying, but respected my silence.

I couldn't tell him I planned on moving out of The Hut. Not yet. That conversation needed to happen face to face, so I could properly express my gratitude. And, because it was also a conversation I didn't think I could get through without breaking down, I grabbed a granola bar from a box I kept in my room and skipped having breakfast in the kitchen. He would wonder. And he would worry. But he would understand soon enough.

The sun shone and I breathed in the constant rhythm of the sea on my way to the massage tables. My schedule was full today and I distracted myself with my work, focusing on muscles and tendons and skin. I couldn't change what was happening to my mom, but I could impact the people on my table. I poured my energy into them, and for a brief period of time, felt peaceful. During a break in the afternoon, I sat down on the beach and called my dad.

He greeted me with concern in his voice. It was a Monday after all, and that meant Dad was hard at work doing God knew what in an office in Houston. Personal calls were a distinct no-no during the week. Always had been. Always would be.

I cut right to the point. "Did you know?"

"Did I know what?" he asked on a heavy sigh. Dad was never one for emotional outbursts and I could hear the warning in his voice. I was five seconds away from his favorite admonishment. *Why don't we table this discussion until you can talk to me like a rational adult?* I heard it my whole life, even when I was an irrational child.

This, however, wasn't a discussion I was willing to

table. "About Mom." The words were a weapon. "Did you know about Mom?"

Dad made a sound I'd never heard him make before, a sharp exhalation that sounded like shock, like pain. "Cat..."

"Did you know Mom had cancer?" I was relentless, pushing through the warning in his voice, the clear cues that meant he didn't want to talk about this now. This was a time for me to take care of my needs. I'd bowed to his for far too long.

There was a pause on the other end of the phone and then, quietly, and with much resignation, he said, "Yes. I knew."

I closed my eyes. His answer felt like betrayal. "Now? Or then?"

"What do you mean?"

I heard the answer in his confusion. He didn't know Mom was sick again, but I pushed forward anyway. "I mean, did you know about the cancer she has now? Or only about the cancer she had then?"

"My God. It's back?" Shock. Disbelief. All the feelings I battled all weekend.

"Yeah. It's back." I explained what I knew in clipped sentences. "And don't you dare tell me to table this conversation until I'm not emotional because I have a damn good reason to be emotional right now. How could you hide this from me?"

"Because she asked me to."

"Since when have you ever thought anything she asked of you made any kind of sense?"

"I loved her once, Cat. I loved her a lot. I don't think I ever stopped loving her."

"How is that supposed to answer my question?" I rubbed my forehead. "Why didn't you tell me?"

"Because she wanted to die knowing you didn't waste your energy worrying about her. She told me she would suffer enough with the illness, she didn't need to add your suffering to hers."

I choked on my exasperation, but Dad continued.

"And it made sense, Catherine. A lot of sense. You were so young and so driven and being a teenager is hard enough without the weight of knowing your mother's life has an impending expiration date."

"So, instead, you lied to me. The two people I trusted more than anything in the world decided that I wasn't strong enough to handle a truth like that and you kept it from me." I closed my eyes as tears pricked, as my voice rose. Their betrayal seethed through me, mixing with my grief, and I had never felt smaller in my life.

"We thought it was for the best. Especially after she started getting better..."

"Well, she's not better now..." I trailed off, letting out a long sigh.

"I'm sorry," Dad said, his grief evident, regret softening the timber of an ever-hard voice. "I'm so sorry."

I paused. Closed my eyes. Took a breath. Rehashing the past would do nothing for the present. "I know," I finally said. And I did. I could hear it in his voice. I knew my father well enough to know that for him to keep something that monumental from me, he had to believe it was for the best. "I just don't know if I'm ready to forgive you yet."

I fully expected him to argue. He wasn't the kind of man to relent, but he let it go. And since we didn't have much more to say to each other, we ended the call with the promise to stay in touch. The rest of the day passed in a frenzy of frustration. For as much as I tried to pour my attention into my clients, I found myself rolling troubled thoughts around in my head.

This cut more deeply than finding Nash in bed with another woman. It dug into my heart and raked itself across my soul. My entire life, the image I'd built of my mother, it was all a lie. Everything about who she was and how I was raised was a façade, one more mask hiding my truth, not only from the world, but from *me*.

At the end of the day, instead of going inside, I sat on the beach and stared at the water. I needed to tell the Huttons I'd be moving out. I needed to sit them down and explain why. I needed to pack up my things and head back to mom's. I needed to be there for her, but I couldn't make myself move because I also needed for none of this to be real.

I felt rooted to the sand, waiting for the vastness of water and sky to make this moment feel insignificant. The sun dipped lower and lower, and I still felt overwhelmed.

The idea of having to explain to the Huttons was bigger than me. Speaking the words to my father was easy because part of me assumed he already knew. Explaining this tragedy to Wyatt or Lucas...I wasn't ready to make it true by taking action. And so, I sat until the sun set and the moon rose. My stomach growled and my head spun.

Footsteps sounded behind me.

I didn't turn.

Didn't want to see anyone.

If I could just have one more minute of silence...

I could wrestle all of this under control...

I'd be able to make sense of it...

I could go inside and move forward...

Just one more minute...

"Cat?"

I recognized Lucas' voice, but I didn't turn to him. Couldn't look at him. I blinked, but kept my focus on the water. He sat down beside me, chest heaving as he fought to catch his breath, sweaty from his evening jog.

"You okay?"

I closed my eyes and sucked in my lips so I couldn't voice the answer. The words would open the floodgates of emotion locked away all day. I wasn't ready. Not now. Not ever. And certainly not in front of him. I sat there like a child, hoping that if I couldn't see him, he couldn't see me and he would give up and go away.

He placed a hand on my shoulder. "Hey," he said, leaning forward to meet my gaze. "You're scaring me. What's wrong?"

His touch proved more than I could handle. The urge to lean in to him, to borrow his strength, to give in to the attraction between us and lose myself in him overwhelmed me. I opened my eyes and tears fell down my cheeks. Lucas cupped my face, wiping the droplets with his thumbs, his gaze boring into my own.

"I'm sorry," I managed, embarrassed that he found me this way, disappointed that I hadn't handled myself with more control.

"For what?"

"For this." I swallowed hard and pulled out of his hands, wiping angrily at my tears.

Lucas took a breath and before he could say anything, I interrupted.

"My mom has cancer." The words felt foreign in my mouth. "Has...had..." I shrugged.

Lucas made a sound like he'd been punched in the gut. I turned to him and the compassion on his face did me in. I told him everything. From learning she'd been sick when she left, to discovering she was sick again. From finding out my dad knew, to wondering what else in my life was built on half-truths and lies. I explained my anger, my fear, the sense of betrayal, and then I had to circle back and explain that on some level, I understood. That my parents wanted to protect me from the harsh reality of our world, and that they only did what they thought was best...

I cried while I spoke, my words pouring out of me in whatever order my thoughts presented themselves, one statement contradicting the next as I saw all the different facets of the problem. Lucas listened as I opened myself to him.

"As you can tell," I said, when I ran out of words. "I'm feeling all the things. I'm confused. I've been trying to process this all day long and obviously haven't gotten very far. And to make it all worse, I feel so selfish for making any of this about me, even a little bit. I'm not the one who's sick. I'm not the one who's going to suffer. How dare I make this about me when my mom needs me to be at my best?"

Lucas wrapped an arm around me and I leaned my head against his shoulder. The warmth of his body invaded mine and I realized I'd grown cold as the sun set. My head ached from all the crying and I wiped at my nose.

"You have every right to feel everything you're feeling," Lucas said, his voice soothing, his breath moving in my hair. "When someone you love is sick, you suffer right along with them." He rubbed his hand along my back and I melted against his strength.

"I'm not ready to say goodbye," I managed. Once again, my words seemed to hold more than one truth. I wasn't ready to say goodbye to Mom, nor was I ready to say goodbye to him.

He nodded, resting his cheek against my head. "I know."

We sat like that for a long time. The tears staining my cheeks dried. A breeze blew in over the ocean and I huddled even closer to him. The buzzing in my brain quieted and finally, my thoughts began to make some kind of sense. "I'm sorry," I said again.

"Don't be. I'm here, Cat." He touched a finger to my chin and lifted my gaze to his. "Right here," he said, his eyes locked on mine. Our faces were inches apart and whatever had been building between us, whatever it was that I'd been trying to ignore, it jumped to life, igniting my body with a deep need for his.

My gaze dropped to his mouth. His lips parted. He leaned in, tilting his head. I angled mine, closing the distance between us. Our noses brushed and the world went quiet, everything dropping away until it was just the two of us, sitting under a moonlit sky, while the ocean licked the sand beneath a blanket of stars.

I needed this kiss. I needed him to obliterate me, to distract me, to take everything bad about this day and make it good again. I needed to breathe him in, to let him in, and I needed him to fill me up so I could finally stop feeling so damn empty.

I leaned in, but Lucas pulled away. "I'm sorry," he said, his voice strangled as he unwrapped his arm from around my shoulder. "I shouldn't..."

He wouldn't look at me, and now it was me who was straining to meet his gaze. "Lucas, it's fine."

He turned to me, something dark and angry glinting in his eyes. "No, it's not."

I tried to explain that he wasn't taking advantage of me, that I wanted to kiss him, that I'd been wanting to kiss him, that I felt like there was something wild and real and important between us, but he shook his head and wouldn't meet my gaze. When I continued, he gripped my shoulders and physically pushed me away.

"Cat. This can't happen." His eyes darted across my face, his pain evident. "There's someone else."

The moment the words were out of his mouth, it looked like he wished he could stuff them right back in. The knowledge that I was almost the other woman sunk like a stone into the pit of my stomach.

I'd had enough. Too many lies. Too many untold

stories. Too much betrayal. Nodding, I stood and opened my mouth, looking for something to say, but there was nothing.

And so, I turned back to the house and walked away while everything inside me raged and screamed.

CHAPTER TWENTY-NINE

LUCAS

I watched Cat fight her way through the sand as she ran away from me. I wanted to chase after her. To pull her into my arms and kiss her until she couldn't see straight. [I couldn't get her out of my head, the feel of her, the sound of her, the pain and sorrow of her admission.

But I didn't move. I sat and watched as she hurried away. As much as it broke my heart to admit, it was time to make a choice. I couldn't keep living between decisions because my choices didn't just affect me. Both the women in my life were caught in the crossfire.

In the weeks since she'd been here, something had grown between Cat and me, something I'd tried to pretend I didn't feel. Something I'd let build. Something I'd seen reflected in the way she looked at me. But it was a something I couldn't let happen because I'd given myself to Katydid, telling her she was worth having, that she was beautiful, that she meant something.

How could I say those things to her, only to turn around and choose Cat? I'd be yet another betrayal and she didn't deserve that. Katydid was such a uniquely wonderful person. I wanted to meet her and hold her and know her. I wanted to sit across from her at crappy burger joints and laugh and talk and explore.

But she was in Galveston and I was here, so I did all those things with Cat instead, letting something develop when I knew better. I couldn't betray Katydid, so instead, I betrayed Cat. I hurt her on a day when she didn't think she could hurt any more than she already did.

I had led her on.

Led them both on.

Hell, I'd led all of us on.

And so, while I wanted to chase Cat down, I didn't. While I wanted to apologize and hold her while she cried, I couldn't. I had to let her go. I had to stop believing I could have both of them.

Both women had been hurt by men they trusted. I

knew that, but let myself develop feelings for them anyway.

Let them develop feelings for me.

The weight of my choices settled onto my shoulders. All of it. Instantly. The reality of what I did sank in and I had never felt like more of an asshole in all my life. How dare I judge Katydid's Nash? I was no better.

My body ached from running. My heart ached from questioning. And my head started pounding with a headache I'd been fighting since Cat avoided me at breakfast this morning. Self-loathing sat on my chest and bile rose in my stomach.

I needed to explain everything to Cat and then I needed to go to Galveston. I needed to see Katydid. I needed to touch her. To feel her. To smell her. I needed to know if she was everything I thought she was. Did she make me feel like I did with Cat? Was the physical attraction as strong as the emotional connection?

It was time to stop living between decisions.

It was time to make a choice.

I only hoped I hadn't made the wrong one.

CHAPTER THIRTY

CAT

My heart pounded its way up my throat as I strode away from Lucas. Nausea boiled in my stomach. When I reached the door to the Hut, my soul begged me to turn and get one last look at him.

Maybe he was coming after me.

Maybe he'd apologize.

Maybe he'd explain.

Maybe he'd sweep me into his arms and tell me that it didn't matter who else there was, because all he wanted was me.

But I didn't turn around. Nor did I stop. I couldn't be with a man who was with someone else. I knew that pain and I would not be the cause of it for another woman.

Anger tightened my hands into fists and I pounded on the porch railing, cursing under my breath when it hurt.

I was mad at Lucas for letting things get as far as they did between us. I was mad at myself for not recognizing how much he wasn't 'just a friend.' I was mad on behalf of the other woman, and guilt churned and burned through me because of Skywalker.

How could I be mad at Lucas, when I was just as guilty?

I yanked open the door and stepped inside, careful to close it quietly behind me in case people were sleeping. I had no idea what time it was, only that the moon was high and my heart was breaking. Life would never be the same after these last few days. How could anything matter ever again after what I'd learned about my mom? What I'd experienced with the people who mattered most to me?

Nash's betrayal had nothing on what I was feeling now. Mom's betrayal. Dad's betrayal. Lucas' betrayal.

And worst of all, my betrayal.

Swimming in guilt, I took a detour through the kitchen to grab a bottle of water, and ran straight into Harlow, her laptop open on the table. She didn't look surprised to see me, nor did she look surprised at my tear-stained face.

"I'm sorry," I mumbled as I lowered my gaze and tried to make my way past her.

She put a hand on my arm. "Hey," she said, her voice gentle. "Do you have a minute?"

I let out a breath. "I really don't..."

"This won't take long." She guided me to the table and pulled out a chair. Reluctantly, I sat. "Listen," she said, her pale blue eyes on mine. "Lucas is a very special kind of person."

The last thing I needed was to talk about how special Lucas was. I was well aware. "Yeah. I know. Look, this isn't a good time," I said as I scooted back in my chair and started to stand.

Harlow put a hand on mine and I froze. "He's loyal to a fault. And despite his gruff exterior, he's the most tenderhearted man you'll ever meet. It's probably that tender heart that makes him so gruff. Defenses and all, you know?"

Despite myself, I nodded and sat back down. Turned out, I knew all about guarding myself against other people.

"I don't know what happened to make you cry," Harlow continued. "But I know my Lucas went out for a late-night run because you'd been avoiding him for the last couple days, so I can take a guess. My brother is attracted to you and it's been a long time since I've seen him so happy around another person. It's just, there's someone else in his life and she was there first."

I snorted. "Thank you, but really. This is none of your business."

"Lucas made a commitment and it can't matter how much he feels for you, he needs to follow through on that commitment. For his own sake."

I narrowed my eyes. "What kind of person do you think I am? I'm not asking him to break his commitment."

"I'm just trying to help you understand…"

"What? That Lucas is special? Believe me, I understand that. Or what? That when you make a commitment to someone, you're supposed to follow through on it? Believe me, I understand that, too. Or at least I thought I did." I stood. "I think your heart's in the right place here, but you are way out of line."

I turned and walked away, but Harlow's next words stopped me in my tracks. "Lucas is in love with you."

I whirled on her. "You do *not* get to say that. You don't get to sit me down and tell me that he's this amazing man who is special and loyal and tender-hearted who also belongs to a different woman. And you most definitely don't get to tell me he loves me. None of this has anything to do with you at all."

"He's my brother."

"And what? You're protecting me from him?"

"No..." Harlow shook her head, confusion puckering her pretty face.

"Oh, you're protecting *him* from *me*?"

"No..." Harlow stood. "This whole situation is confusing for him. I'm just asking you to be patient."

I let out a bitter laugh. "I am tired of being patient while other people work through their problems. I'm tired of sitting back and letting everyone else mean more than I do." I stepped back, disgust curling the corners of my lips while her words bounced around my skull.

Lucas is in love with you...

...in love with you...

...love...

That still-small voice rejoiced while my heart broke in two. In love with me or not, I still wasn't enough for him. Whatever that flaw inside me was, regardless as to how much I thought I was hiding it from him, he saw it. He was in love with me, but he chose someone else. He didn't even have the decency to tell me about her until the moment I needed him the most.

This whole day had been nothing but lies and loss, deceit and betrayal. I was suddenly exhausted and desperate for solitude.

I started for the stairs, but somehow, I sensed him.

Moments before the back door opened, I knew Lucas was near. The urge to turn and run into the safety of his arms was so strong, I couldn't move until I heard the door latch quietly behind him. With one last withering look at Harlow, I forced myself out of the kitchen. Took the stairs one step at a time as hushed voices and heated conversation sounded behind me. Let myself into my room, sent Mom a text explaining where I was, sat down on my bed, and waited for morning.

CHAPTER THIRTY-ONE

FROM: Katydid <getoveryourself@imail.com>
to: Skywalker
<themanwhofoundyourjournal@imail.com>
date: September 6, 2018 at 7:45 am
subject: Goodbye, Skywalker

I'm not in Texas anymore. I haven't been for weeks now. After Nash left me, I had nowhere to go, so I moved in with my mom. She lives in the Florida Keys. In an RV. Which means I had to sleep on a bed that was also our table. I got a job at a resort as a masseuse, and oddly enough, they offer housing to employees who need a place to stay. I moved in and have been living here almost the entire time we've been emailing.

I didn't tell you.

Why? I still don't know.

I think I liked the anonymity.

That little bit of a buffer between us after everything that happened between me and Nash.

Or maybe I didn't want you to find out I was so far away because I was afraid you'd stop emailing if you thought we would never meet. Maybe I wanted to keep you even though I never really had you. Maybe the only way I could be completely open with you was to know I was still in control.

Honestly, I can't explain why I didn't tell you, why I felt the need to keep you close, but separate. All I know is that I did.

The question I have though, is do *you* know why *you* did?

Why you told me everything but your name?

Your occupation?

You mentioned a family once. Are you married? Is that why you never responded after I dropped a major hint that I was ready to meet in person?

Anyway, my name is Catherine Wallace. My friends call me Cat. I'm a masseuse who is too afraid to start her own business even though she claims that's her lifelong goal. A woman who is too afraid of being rejected that she hides behind half-truths and is more than happy to take the attention a stranger offered her.

The thing is, you're not giving me enough. Which

is a shitty thing to say, because I'm not giving you enough either. But I need a real person. One who can look me in the eyes and laugh with me and call me on my bullshit.

I met a man, Skywalker. And, for a while, I thought I was falling in love with you, but then I realized what it felt like to fall in love with someone for real. Someone I can touch. Smell. Hear. Someone I don't have time to cultivate my answers for, someone whose very existence challenges me to be real. Honest.

And I've not been very honest. Everything I gave to you, I kept from him. Everything I kept from you, I gave to him.

I think you are one of the most amazing human beings to ever walk this earth. A man with integrity and humor and a poetic way of looking at the world. In any other situation, we could have been wonderful together. But in this situation, I'm going to have to call it.

I can't keep doing this.

Living in my head. Falling in love with you when I actually don't know anything about your life. This isn't right. It's...I don't know...I'm not being real and I very much believe that I need to be real or I'll end up in another situation like the one I was in with Nash.

The other man doesn't love me, by the way. Or

maybe he does, at least according to his sister. But there's someone else.

Anyway, this is a verbal vomit of confusion. In some ways, you've become my best friend, the one person I pour my heart out too, and so, how can I NOT explain this to you. When I discovered Nash had been cheating on me, it hurt. My God. It hurt so much. And you and I aren't in a relationship, and maybe I've placed too much importance on who we are for each other, but the truth of it is, I can't be like Nash. I can't keep part of myself from you while giving it to someone else because what if, *what if*, you are falling in love with me too?

What if you spend every day at the coffee shop, waiting for me to walk through the door?

And I'm across the Gulf of Mexico, slowly falling in love with a man who belongs to someone else.

It's a tragedy, Skywalker. It's a damn tragedy.

CHAPTER THIRTY-TWO

LUCAS

My phone vibrated, drawing me from sleep in time to hear Cat's door closing and her soft footsteps disappearing down the hall. She was leaving without saying goodbye and I was going to let her.

I *had* to let her.

As much as it hurt, I had to let her go. It was time to give myself completely to Katydid. Today, I would send an email, a formal introduction, and ask to meet her in our coffee shop.

Wiping sleep out of my eyes, I rolled over and swiped my phone off my nightstand. The sorrow I felt because Cat was leaving diminished when I saw Katydid's name, only to surge back to life when I saw the subject line.

Goodbye, Skywalker.

Goodbye?

Goodbye?

I turned my back on Cat on her worst day for Katydid. And only after that, she hit me with goodbye? I unlocked my phone and read through the email, then sat there, stunned.

I read it again.

I would have read it again, if I hadn't realized that Cat was downstairs, packing up her Jeep as I sat there like an idiot, processing the biggest shock of my life.

Cat was Katydid.

Katydid was Cat.

I could have them both.

As long as I could get downstairs before she left.

Clutching my phone to my chest, I ran down the stairs in my bare feet and gray sweats, taking them two at a time and rushing past a groggy Wyatt on my way out the door.

There she was, the wind from an incoming storm whipping her hair around her face as she struggled to get the top back on her Jeep. She was crying. I could see it in the way she held herself. I called her name, but she turned her back to me. She wanted me to leave her alone.

But I couldn't. With my heart yammering in my chest, I took off across the parking lot. "Katydid!"

She froze. And then, slowly, she lowered her arms and turned to face me as the first few drops of rain splashed dark spots onto the pavement. A lock of hair blew across her face and I moved to brush it away. She stepped back and swiped it away herself.

"What did you call me?"

"Katydid." I held out my phone as if it explained everything. "I read your email."

"What email?" Cat scowled, her eyes darkening with suspicion.

"The one you sent me before you left."

"But I didn't send you..." Like clouds moving to reveal the sun, confusion left her face. "Are you Skywalker?"

The only words I could muster were, "Can you believe it?"

"*You're* Skywalker?"

I nodded. "I am."

I expected her to smile. To laugh. To talk about the crazy coincidences that brought us together. I expected her to ask questions, probably the same questions buzzing through my own head.

She did none of those things.

Her eyebrows drew together. Her eyes narrowed. Her jaw clenched.

I waited for her to come to terms with everything, but she only kept looking angrier. So I did the thing any rational man would do in a situation like this. I cupped her face in my hands and kissed her as if my life depended on it.

All the feelings I'd built for Katydid were in that kiss. All the physical attraction for Cat. All the pent-up frustration of wanting both of them but not really having either of them went into that single moment of contact. I ran my hands along her back, savoring her curves and obliterating the space between us.

Cat pulled back, confusion still dancing with anger. She slapped me across the face, then dropped her jaw, stunned by her own action.

"Cat..."

She slapped me again. Then stepped into my arms and kissed me.

Her body melted against mine, as soft and supple as I knew it would be. Her hands slid up my arms as her lips parted for me. She gave me her soul with that kiss, and I gladly took it all, cherishing the gift for the treasure it was.

This woman was meant for me. As our tongues clashed in the parking lot, the wind rioting around my bare shoulders as her soft breasts pressed against my chest, I realized that with her, I could have everything. Another person with her eyes open, willing to question the way she saw the world, to look at everything from as many different angles as she could think of. She was here. In my arms.

I didn't have to worry about two different women, because both of them were wrapped up into one magnificent human being.

A raindrop hit my shoulder. First one. Then another. And another. Cat pulled back, smiling, as the skies opened up. She laughed as her hair matted to her head and her T-shirt clung to her pert breasts.

I swept her into my arms and carried her back to the house, pushing right past a very surprised looking Wyatt, and climbed the steps to deposit her on my bed. She was mine. She was everything.

And I was going to show her what it meant to have her body worshipped by a man who knew what he was doing.

CHAPTER THIRTY-THREE

CAT

Nerves spun in my stomach as Lucas undressed me, reverently peeling back my wet clothing as if I was the greatest gift he had ever received. I wanted this. I wanted it so badly, I hadn't been able to fall asleep at night, knowing he was on the other side of the wall. That sexy body wrapped in sheets and who knew what else.

Lucas trailed kisses along my throat as his hands cupped my breasts and his knees spread my thighs. Anxiety quenched the fire burning inside me and I scurried out from underneath him. I was broken. My body hadn't responded to stimulation in years, and as stimulating as Lucas was, fear trembled through my limbs. What if, after all we'd been through, I still couldn't perform?

"Lucas..." I began, unsure where I intended to end.

Of all the people in my world, this man knew what I had been struggling through better than anyone. In email after email, I had poured my heart out to him. I watched him understand my fear and then I saw a glimpse of the cocky, self-assured man who left that first note in my journal. His gaze strengthened and a predatory look settled across his face. In response, a low thrum started in my core—more than I had felt in years.

My muscles clenched.

My breath quickened.

And Lucas smiled.

"I've got you," he murmured, brushing a strand of hair off my face. "Trust me, KatyCat."

Happiness bloomed in me, hearing the new nickname, and I stared at the man who was the perfect blend of everything I thought I could never have.

Lucas placed a finger under my chin, lifting my face to his. "I promised you that I would bring you ecstasy and I will. I will, Cat. Close your eyes. Stop thinking. Just feel."

I did as he asked, closing my eyes, focusing on the sensation of his skin against mine, on the whisper of his breath as he kissed my skin. The faint hint of his cologne danced through the air between us. The stubble along his chin scratched deliciously down my stomach as he lowered himself, kissing and biting and licking and sucking. His hands pressed on my inner thighs, spreading me wide, opening me to him.

I tensed, ready to stop him before he could start, and then his tongue flicked out, drawing a delicate line across my slit. I dropped my head back, moaning. His touch was decadent, working my body with a delicate patience, driving me forward with a relentless rhythm.

I threaded my fingers through his hair as he worked his magic. Carefully, and with much attention to detail, Lucas brought me back to life. Awakening parts of me I had forgotten existed.

Sensation washed over me, humming and thrumming. I lost sight of where we were and who we were. All the fear and anxiety I kept locked inside melted away, as inch by frozen inch thawed.

I screamed his name as my breath hitched and my hips bucked, hands clutching at the sheets.

His rhythm never faltered, though I felt him smile against me as he slipped a finger inside, stroking and tracing my inner walls. Just like that, an orgasm exploded through my nerve-endings. Fireworks danced through my vision and my body melted as I moaned, low and primal. I arched my back, tightening my lips against the sound, aware that we weren't the only people in the house.

As my body writhed under Lucas' ministrations, he guided me over the edge and then right back to it time and again. With my legs trembling and shaking, I lifted my head and stared down at his blonde hair between my thighs. He sat up, drawing the back of his hand across his mouth as he stood, his gaze raking over me. I smiled sheepishly, feeling languid and sated and ready for more.

In one swift movement, Lucas freed himself of his sweatpants and then pulled a condom from his bedside table. I had only a few stuttering heartbeats to appreciate him in all his glory before he gripped his thick length in one hand, guiding it toward my spread legs. He pressed his tip against me and I ran my fingernails along his soldier's body mottled with scars.

As I met his glorious blue eyes, I realized that I had belonged to him all along.

My mom and dad being such opposites...

My childhood happening in three perfect chunks of parenting...

My life had molded me for this man who was so strong and stable on the outside, but so soft and wonderful in his heart. My warrior poet.

Lucas smiled down at me as he slipped inside, the pressure of his girth enough to bring a second orgasm out of nowhere. It shattered over me as he rolled his hips and whispered my name. I grabbed his arms, holding on to him as he moved. Clinging to him as if he could keep me tethered to the earth while my soul soared somewhere high above.

"You're everything," he whispered. "Everything I ever wanted. Everything I ever needed and never thought I'd have."

Before I could reply, his eyelids fluttered closed and pleasure washed over his face. He gripped my hips and plunged into me, sending me over the edge once again as our bodies rioted in unison.

CHAPTER THIRTY-FOUR

LUCAS

I lowered myself to the bed beside Cat. She rolled onto her side, her face just inches from mine. "Hi," she said, emotion swimming in her eyes.

I smiled as I traced a finger along her hairline. "Hi."

"So, how did..." I began at the same time she said, "I can't believe..."

A knock sounded at the door before either of us could continue. "Ummm...Cat?" Laughter framed Wyatt's voice. "I just wanted to let you know that I finished putting the top on your Jeep. It's still raining, but you...uh...don't need to stop what you're doing. Or worry about the rest of us. We didn't hear a thing."

Cat sat up, clutching the sheets to her chest,

looking absolutely appalled. She pressed a hand to her open mouth, eyes wide. "I'll never be able to look your family in the eyes again." She glanced around the room. "This is all there is for me. I'll never be able to leave. I'll just be stuck in your bed for the rest of eternity."

I laughed and pulled her back into my arms, thrilled to finally be able to touch her, still struggling to reconcile the fact that she was both women I had come to adore. "Works for me," I said, then deposited kisses along her jawline before capturing her lips with mine. She tasted of honey—sweet and rich and wonderful.

"I just can't believe you're...you." I murmured the words against her ear and Cat nodded her agreement.

"I keep trying to make sense of it, but it just feels like magic."

"Like, kismet."

"Serendipity." Cat smiled, tracing a finger along my cheek. "I figured it out. Once. On the boat, the day I asked about your scars? You talked about dying, and having a nickname. For a few seconds, I couldn't breathe. Not even a little bit. I was so sure you were Skywalker. But then Wyatt called you the Bionic Man and I realized what an idiot I was to think..." Cat trailed off, wonder dancing in her eyes. "I think I sent you—the Skywalker you—an email after that."

I tried to think back over the last several weeks,

weaving the timeline of Cat and Katydid together into one tapestry of moments. "Was that the one where you talked about the masks we wear?"

"I don't know. Maybe?"

"That email stood out to me for two reasons. For one, you used the word intense, and I can't tell you how many times people have used that word to describe me. And two, it was the first time you ever sounded anything but happy since we started talking."

"If I used the word intense, I was surely talking about you." Cat paused, weeks of emotion on her face. "If it's the one I'm thinking of, I had started to realize how much chemistry we had, and was really doubting...well...everything. The attraction between us, both in email and in real life, was so powerful. And there I was, trying to work out how to choose between you."

"I completely understand," I said, then pulled her into my arms. I'd been wading through similar concerns, wondering how I could be falling in love with two women at once, when loyalty was such a core tenet of my personality. It seemed too good to be true to learn that I had actually been falling in love with just one woman. One beautiful, amazing, intelligent, sexy woman.

I said as much to Cat and she blushed, her cheeks warming until they were adorably pink, her eyes sparkling like the clearest waters in Caleb's cove. And then, the light in her dimmed, slowly fading out until sadness tugged at her features. "I hate that I have to go. It's almost cruel that I have to leave after all this."

"Go? Go where?" I just got her. I didn't think I could let her go.

"My mom is expecting me. I told her I'd be back last night, but was such a wreck, I couldn't bring myself to face her. To face anyone really. I just sat there on the beach, feeling sorry for myself until you showed up. I need to call her, in case she's worrying."

Cat fished her cell out of the back pocket of her shorts and perched on the edge of my bed, wrapped in a sheet and more stress than seemed possible for her to bear. I heard her mom answer with a joyous "There's my Katydid!" and was once again struck by how close we must have come to stumbling upon the truth so many times.

Cat apologized for being late, then tossed me a glance, a smile tugging at her lips, juxtaposing the slump of her shoulders and bowed head. "You're never going to believe what happened," she said then paused while her mother replied. "No. Not that." She listened, then laughed lightly. "Not that either, but you're getting warmer. Remember my problem with the men? Well..."

Cat launched into an explanation of what had transpired this morning, quite conveniently skipping over the part that led to her wearing nothing but my bedsheets. She laughed again, with more weight behind it, then promised she was all packed up and would be out of here soon. Her gaze turned to me, confusion twisting her brows together. "She wants to talk to you," she said, then punched the speakerphone button.

"Lucas?" Cat's mom sounded like she was smiling.

"Speaking," I replied, falling back on formality.

"Oh, Cat! That voice! If the rest of him is even half that delicious then I understand every dirty thought you've had..."

Cat groaned and sucked in her lips. "Is there maybe something else you'd like to talk about? Something less embarrassing?"

Cat's mom introduced herself as Angela Wallace and the humor in her voice wasn't lost on me. I would guess, Angela enjoyed watching her daughter blush as much as I did. "I'm going to ask you something, Lucas," she continued. "But first, I want to make sure you're aware that I'm dying of cancer."

Cat gasped. "Mom!"

Angela kept right on talking, despite her daughter's evident dismay. "As a Marine, I can only assume that honor means a great deal to you. Let me remind you that you would have to be particularly cruel not to honor a dying woman's wish."

The smile I heard in her voice settled it. I really liked Angela Wallace. It took a lot of courage to look death in the face and turn it into a joke. "I'm not a cruel man, ma'am. Your wish is my command."

"Good. Then here's what I want. I want you and my daughter to spend the next week completely wrapped up in each other. I don't want you to think about me. I don't want you to talk about me. And I certainly don't want you to come see me."

"Mom..." Cat shook her head. "You know I can't do that..."

"I'm not going anywhere yet, Katydid. And having you here, chasing after me with glasses of water and worried eyes isn't going to do me any good, especially when I know you could be spending the time with your seething warrior."

I guffawed as Cat fell back onto the bed, her cheeks on fire with embarrassment. "I cannot believe you said that." She widened her eyes as she stared at the ceiling. "Wait. Yep. I totally can believe you said that." She glanced at me, an apology written on her face.

I took her hand in mine and gave it a squeeze. "Seething warrior. Intense and glowery. I get it. Nothing I haven't heard before." I reiterated my promise to Cat's mom who thanked me, then asked to speak to her daughter in private. Cat turned off the speakerphone, then pressed the device to her ear and listened to whatever her mom had to say. In the end, Cat promised to stay with me for a week, then ended the call with a sigh.

She sat on the edge of the bed, staring at her phone. "I can't decide how I'm feeling right now. There's just so much to process. Between learning why my mom left in the first place, back when I was a kid. To discovering my time with her is limited. To thinking I was being despicable, cheating on two men I respected more than I thought possible. To finding out that somehow, *somehow*, both of those men were you...I can't decide if I should laugh or cry."

I gathered her in my arms, cradling her like the angel she was, and lowered her back onto the bed. "Feel it all," I said, kissing first one eyelid, then the other. "Feel everything." I kissed her petal-soft lips. "But for now, just feel this." I took her hand and lowered it to my straining erection.

Her eyes fluttered open, staring wide into mine, before she took me at my word and felt everything I had to offer.

Twice.

CHAPTER THIRTY-FIVE

Cat

We finally ventured out of Lucas' room around dinner time and were met by Harlow, who regarded us with a look of stern disappointment.

"I know what you're thinking," Lucas said to his sister, "but you have it all wrong."

Harlow held up her hands, throwing a cold look my way. "None of this is my business and it's not my place to judge."

"You're right. It's not." Lucas smirked. "But you still have it all wrong." He launched into an explanation of what we discovered this morning and astonishment grew on Harlow's face.

"You're kidding me!" Her gaze bounced between

us, looking for the *gotcha* to our story. "You're not kidding. Oh. Oh, wow! This is..." She shook her head. "I couldn't sell that idea to a publisher if I tried."

Lucas and I spent the evening making the strangest dinner out of things we found in the kitchen, laughing as we assembled the meal. Whenever Lucas came close, he touched me, trailing a finger along my cheek. Bumping his hip against mine. Pulling me into an embrace and kissing me as if he were a dying man savoring his last breath. We ate the odd assortment of food in his room, insulating ourselves from the watchful eyes and secret smiles of his family. They were happy for us, but we weren't ready to share this with anyone yet. It all felt too new. Too surreal. Too impossible.

I spent the night in Lucas' bed, wrapped in his arms and the incredulity of the day. Neither of us slept well, though that had more to do with our inability to leave each other alone than anything. We reveled in the connection, touching and kissing and talking and making love. I was careful to stay quiet, ever aware of the rest of his family on the other side of the thin walls. And, while everything he did felt amazing, and I felt more pleasure with him than I ever had with Nash, the fact that I had to pay enough attention to stay quiet completely contained the passion of our lovemaking. It was beautiful, but careful, and we could both feel the difference.

The next morning, I had a string of clients lined up until lunchtime. I snuck out of his bed, careful not to disturb him, then showered, did my hair, and got dressed—all while lost in deep thought. Two days ago, my world had made sense. I understood how things worked. My mom was eccentric and my dad enjoyed rules. I had two different men who satisfied the two different parts of me that would never be in agreement.

Today, my mom wasn't eccentric, she was sick.

My dad enjoyed his rules, but I suspected they were a safety net, many of them put in place after losing mom.

And the two men I thought I loved were actually one man—one wonderful, perfect man who I desperately wished I could climb back into bed with.

My world was on its side and I had no idea how to move forward. Mom's words to Lucas kept playing through my thoughts.

...you would have to be particularly cruel not to honor a dying woman's wish...

Sometimes those words were a cold dash of reality. Other times, they made me smile. Even facing the end of her life, my mother had a sense of humor. And more, even knowing she was looking at a bleak future, she was protecting me, trying to make me happy despite her pain. It was a razor's edge of love, bitter and sweet, difficult and pure. It filled me up and cut so deeply, I had to look away from the thoughts or I would drift off, awash in too many emotions to name.

Once again, I lost myself in flesh and bone, pouring my energy into my clients. Softening knotted muscles. Pinpointing pain spots and working them until they gave way. Throughout it all, flashes of Lucas would enter my mind and I would smile until my face hurt.

When lunch arrived, I took the quickest path back to The Hut, hoping to find Lucas waiting for me in the kitchen. As I turned a corner, a hand shot out and grabbed my wrist. I yelped as I found myself face to face with my seething warrior, who slowly backed me against the wall of a bungalow, his eyes burning into mine. He kissed me as the wind blew in off the ocean and all the turmoil of the day rushed out to sea.

"I couldn't wait to see you," he murmured, stealing kisses as if making up for lost time.

"Same," I managed. "I was hurrying back to the kitchen. Hoping to find you there."

"I saw. You should be more aware of your surroundings. Anyone can sneak up on you when you're distracted like that."

"Noted," I said, unable to fight the massive smile breaking across my face.

Lucas looked stern. "I feel like you should be more

concerned, KatyCat. There was a man lurking in the shadows, thinking about doing terrible things to you, and not only did you fail to notice him, but he managed to sneak up and grab you."

"Terrible thoughts, huh?" I pressed my body against his, aware of his erection straining between us. "Like what, exactly?"

"That information is classified." Lucas nibbled at my ear, trailing his hands under my shirt. "But if you knew, you wouldn't be so comfortable where you are right now."

"You should try me. You might be surprised."

Lucas made a sound, half moan, half growl. It was the single hottest thing I had ever heard in my life and I made it my mission to hear it as often as I could from that point forward. Approaching footsteps caught my attention and I stepped away from this man who could undo me so completely in the space of a few minutes. An older couple meandered into view.

"Anything else, Mr. Hutton?" I asked in what I hoped was my most professional voice.

Lucas scowled. "Actually, yes. There is something I'd like to discuss with you, but it can wait. I'll speak to you later, Ms. Wallace."

The woman caught my eye and offered a smile that said we hadn't fooled her one bit, but she wasn't going to blow our cover. She threaded her hand into her husband's, and they disappeared from view. I watched Lucas stride away and wondered why he wasn't going to have lunch with me. That thought disappeared as I made my way into the kitchen. A giant bouquet of flowers covered the table where I normally sat. Harlow, Caleb, and Eli smirked while Wyatt shook his head. No one said a word as I read the card.

KatyCat-

As ecstatic as I am to have you, I want to have you completely and I think we both realized that can't happen here, where I have to share you with my family. I have a surprise for you. Pack a bag. We leave tomorrow. Even the moon envies your beauty.

Lucas

I ran a finger along the card, smiling at Skywalker's way with words combining with Lucas' intensity. When I looked up, the Huttons laughed at me.

"It's not like we didn't see this coming a mile away," Wyatt said. "I just wasn't prepared for Hurricane Lucas to hit so hard."

Eli shot his brother a look. "Really? When has Hurricane Lucas *not* hit this hard?"

Caleb laughed his agreement and I frowned at Harlow.

"Everything he does is extreme," she explained. "Nothing is a half-measure with Luc. It's a beautiful thing." She smiled and placed her hand on mine. "Truly beautiful."

***

Chris Magic was in rare form tonight after hearing my story. "You're telling me that you didn't just find the best job of all the best jobs, but you also managed to fall in love with some hot Marine with a wealthy family?" His face loomed on the screen as he leaned in close to the camera to make a point. "And you didn't even think, not for one itty-bitty moment, that I deserved to know this was going on? Not even a little bit?"

"I kind of wanted to keep it quiet. I didn't know what I was going to do, and I thought I'd wait to tell the story until I had a chance to figure it all out."

"That's the problem with you, Kitty. You're always thinking. Never feeling. You hold yourself too close."

"Maybe."

"Maybe, she says." Chris' image lurched as he picked up his laptop and plopped dramatically onto his sofa. "What you mean is, gee Chris, you're right. I should have told you all of this sooner so I didn't have to go so long torturing myself by thinking I was falling in love with two men."

Chris' energy was everything I needed, soothing my frazzled nerves with his penchant for drama. "Is that right? Telling you would have solved everything, huh?"

"Sure would."

"And how's that?"

"I would have told you to stop playing games and give your mystery man your name already. And then I would have told you to explain to Lucas exactly what you were feeling. And boom. Problem solved. Torture over. But no. You had to go around, doing it the hard way."

I smiled because he was right. The whole debacle would have ended much sooner if I had done it his way. But would I have given so much of my inner thoughts to Skywalker if I knew he was Lucas? And would I have held myself back from Lucas because it was too soon after Nash and I wasn't interested in falling in love ever again? Maybe things unfolded exactly as they needed to, in order for Lucas and me to end up together and happy.

Thoughts of my mom encroached on the word *happy*. How could I be happy when she was dying? But I dutifully pushed those thoughts away before I could think too long. Mom was right. She wasn't going anywhere anytime soon—in fact, she might not be going anywhere at all. She had already beaten this once. Who was to say she wouldn't do it again? Regardless, the least I could do was try and honor her wish by focusing on myself for a little bit.

"Found it," Chris said.

"Found what?"

"The perfect dress for your little getaway." He leaned closer to the camera as he studied something on his screen and his face filled my view. "There, I sent you the link. Revel in its glory, bitch."

I clicked on the link and my jaw dropped. It really was perfect. Cream-colored and full length, with spaghetti straps and a plunging neckline. Dressy enough to walk into any restaurant, and casual enough not to look out of place on the beach. "It's gorgeous!"

"And with your red hair and creamy skin, that sexy Marine won't know what hit him." Thankfully, the dress was available nearby and after apologizing to my friend five more times for not telling him all the details of my sordid story as they were happening, I drove myself to the store and tried it on. Chris was right. I had never felt so beautiful.

Even the moon envies your beauty.

I smiled like a goon at my reflection and didn't stop until I was back at The Hut, carefully packing up my bag for tomorrow, wondering what Lucas had in mind.

CHAPTER THIRTY-SIX

Lucas

It had taken some work to get reservations to Morada Bay's sold out Full Moon Party. But, once they realized I was Burke Hutton's son, they made sure to get me the best possible room at The Moorings—their host hotel— and two tickets to the celebration on the beach. For the first time in a long time, I was glad to be part of my father's legacy.

Cat gave me the side-eye when we pulled up in front of the hotel, which also offered isolated bunga- lows that didn't share a wall with anyone. "A hotel?" she asked. "Weren't we just at a hotel?"

I could have rented one of the bungalows at The Hut for Cat and me to find some privacy, but we would still have to face my siblings and their knowing glances in the kitchen. The first time Cat and I were together, she was unhindered, crying out with abandon as I thrust into her. Since then, while our physical chemistry was still unmatched, I could feel her holding back. I could almost kill Wyatt for knocking on the door that morning, though if the situation had been reversed, I probably would have done the same thing.

So, while on paper, it was maybe a little strange to move from one hotel to another, it made sense when taking the details into consideration. I wanted to make Cat feel special. I wanted to take her somewhere beautiful. To celebrate what we'd found in each other. To take her mind off her mother. And to make good on my promise to bring her the pleasure she had missed for so long with that Nash character.

And for that, we needed privacy.

The day I read her journal, falling partly in love with her on the basis of her words alone, I swore to Cat that I would do everything in my power to worship her, to transport her, to make sure she felt all the pleasure she was designed for.

A woman's body was a Ferrari, designed to feel sensation so deeply, it opened her heart. Under the right hands, a woman could experience near constant pleasure, orgasm blending into orgasm blending into orgasm, until her legs shook, her body trembled, and her soul caught fire.

Most men weren't equipped to handle a Ferrari.

I wanted to learn Cat's body, to understand all the things that made her writhe under me, falling further and further out of control. I couldn't do that if she was too focused on being quiet. She couldn't lose herself while clutching at her mouth, swallowing her moans. I needed her wild and untethered so I could follow through on the promise I made all those weeks ago. A promise left in a stranger's journal.

I gave her a silent smile as we hopped out of the Jeep. Even when she continued to question, I stayed quiet. She would understand soon enough.

The moment the door to our room closed behind us, I swept her into my arms, kissing her as if I could devour her. She moaned against my mouth and the sound went straight to my cock. I threaded a hand in her hair and pulled, forcing her to look at the ceiling while I nipped and sucked around her jaw. "Mine," I murmured.

Cat rolled her hips in silent agreement, pressing against my erection. My need for her caught fire and I almost lost sight of my mission in my desire to have her hard and have her now. I gripped her ass and lifted. She wrapped her legs around my waist and, in a war of tongues and teeth, we made our way to the bed.

"Undress," I ordered as I worked the button of my pants.

Cat obeyed, licking her lips as she eyed me hungrily. After our clothes fell to the floor in a heap, I gathered her wrists in my hand and pinned them above her head. She swallowed another gasp as I took her nipple past my lips.

"No one can hear us," I said. "Give yourself to me. Let go, Cat."

Understanding drew a slow smile across her face and the next time I touched her, she moaned low and long. After that, I drove her body the way it was designed to be driven. Bringing her to the brink of pleasure time and again, sometimes letting her fall into an orgasm, sometimes letting the orgasm fall away before calling it back to life again. As my cock throbbed with need, I watched ecstasy transform Cat's face.

Her cries grew louder and more insistent. My name echoed off the walls. Obscenities and prayers spilled past her lips, and then she lost the ability to form words at all. When all she could manage were soft whimpers and desperate moans, I buried my cock inside her warm wetness, making a sound so low and primal, I didn't recognize it.

Her eyes sprung open. "Yes!" she gasped. The moment I moved, another orgasm flooded her body. Her head dropped back and her inner walls clenched around my dick. I gripped her hips and drove into her as sweat dripped down my back, and I came harder than I ever remembered coming in my life.

When Cat stepped out of the bathroom, all I could do was stare. Her hair hung around her shoulders in soft waves. A dress clung to her body and draped to the floor, accentuating the feminine perfection of her curves. While she typically wore very little makeup, tonight she had done something to her eyes to make them stand out like gems in her face.

Her smile faltered. "What?" She glanced down. "No good? Too much? I can change..."

"It's perfect." I stood and crossed the room. "You're perfect."

"The way you stared at me, I thought I'd done something wrong."

"Oh, no. Everything about you is right."

CHAPTER THIRTY-SEVEN

CAT

While Lucas showered and dressed, I took another moment to fuss with my hair in the mirror. The way he had looked at me, like I was his entire world, it set butterflies moving through my stomach and happiness coursing through my bloodstream. I imagined it as golden energy, infiltrating my muscles, my bones, my cells. I had always wanted someone to look at me like that. As if I were an angel, a gift.

At first, I thought I had it all wrong, the dress, the hair. Too fancy. Not fancy enough. He had just glared, so intense, so strong, but then something soft and wonderful had settled into his eyes and I realized that he liked what he saw. That was my Lucas, intense and glowery and so overwhelming I could barely think.

An urge to reach out to mom had me swiping my phone off the table, but after remembering our promise to her, I shot a pic of me in the dress to Chris instead. His response left me shaking my head and promising to invite more magic into my life.

When Lucas emerged from the bathroom, wearing a white button down tucked into black slacks, his sleeves rolled up to display his corded forearms, it was my turn to stare.

"Wow...are you really mine?" I asked.

Lucas grinned. "Completely."

He took my hand, twirled me around, then pulled me into his arms, swaying as he hummed silently—a slow dance for just the two of us, silent and sated in our room.

We ate dinner at Pierre's—a fabulous restaurant down the street. The food was good and the conversation was better. I had more wine than I intended and laughed more than I had in longer than I could remember.

As the waiter cleared our dessert plates, I leaned forward. "Thank you for such a wonderful evening," I said to Lucas.

"We're not done yet. The moon hasn't had a chance to envy your beauty."

I gave him a funny look and he laughed. "Of all the ways I imagined you—when I was Skywalker falling in love with Katydid—never, in my wildest dreams could I have imagined you as perfect as you are."

I blushed, then remembered the day I tried to unfreeze my numb nether regions by imagining Skywalker, only to keep coming up with images of Lucas. Of how we ran into each other in the hallway moments later and I had to try and navigate the conversation knowing I had almost solved my own problem while imagining him at the wheel. I considered telling the story, but decided against it as embarrassment stole my words.

Lucas noticed the blush coloring my cheeks and I found myself explaining it anyway. A wicked smile lit his face as his eyes simmered with lust. "You might have to reenact that for me tonight."

My blush deepened and I made some demure excuse, but Lucas leaned forward. "That wasn't a request, KatyCat." The stern edge in his voice set my desire on fire and I was suddenly very eager to be back in our room. Instead, Lucas led me outside. The sun had just set and the sky burned against the sea. We followed music and laughter toward a throng of people.

"Welcome to Morada Bay's Full Moon Party," Lucas said as we passed three men dancing to tribal drums. We drank. We danced. We laughed. Time stood still as we lost ourselves in each other.

On that night, there was no sickness. No past. No present. Nothing to worry about. Nothing to fear. It was just the two of us, content to be together. Happy. Whole. And unconcerned with the rest of the world.

At least for a little while.

We spent the next few days as if we were an island. The two of us adrift in our happiness with nothing around us for miles. We drank too much. We slept too late. We explored our bodies, our hearts, our minds. It was a crash course in all things Cat and Lucas and I couldn't have asked for anything more. But as the days dwindled away, I grew evermore aware that the real world was waiting for us. That this week would end and we would go back to The Hut. He would stay there, and I would go stay with Mom.

I would have to face the reality of losing her. Of watching her grow sick. Of watching her body fail. I'd have to balance my need to be with her with my need to be with Lucas and I wasn't sure I could manage that with any grace. I wasn't ready to lose my mom. Could I do it without pushing Lucas away?

At first, Lucas ignored my darkening moods, and I

was grateful for that, but after a while, I wished I could talk about what was bothering me. As if he could sense my need, he sat down next to me on the beach one day. Took my hand. And as we stared at the waves crashing along the shore, said, "I know she made me promise not to let you think about her. But I know you well enough to know that you couldn't stop worrying about your mom, no matter how hard you tried. Your heart is too big not to fill it with the people that matter to you." He turned to me. "I'm here, if you want to talk."

And talk I did. I shared every fear. Every worry. Every question that had cropped up since learning Mom was sick. I told him she didn't want to seek treatment and I explained how torn I was because of her decision. "On one hand, I get it. The medication is almost as bad as the cancer itself. And she already went into remission once, so what are the chances of beating it again? So, if she wants to skip as much of the suffering as she can, I understand. But on the other hand, if there's something we can do to give her a better chance of surviving, then damn it. I want to do it. Because she *did* beat it once. Maybe that means she can do it again."

Lucas nodded thoughtfully. "I think both of your reactions are completely normal." A wave rolled up to kiss our feet, depositing sea foam on the sand. After some time, he turned to me. "What if you didn't have to move out of The Hut?"

I had been afraid this conversation was coming, though had hoped he would understand me enough not to push. "Lucas..." I turned to him, but my explanation died away at the excitement on his face.

"And what if there was a way to ease your mom's suffering at the same time?"

"You have my attention."

Lucas explained that his mom had been wanting to explore the health and wellness side of the resort for a long time. "A lot of it's in place already, the massage, the food, the meditation..."

"You want to move my mom into The Hut?"

Lucas nodded. "I can't imagine anyone would have a problem with that. And while I wouldn't go expecting any miracles, at least she would be surrounded by people who cared. And taken care of to the best of our ability."

Gratitude brought tears to my eyes. The thought of having mom at The Hut, where the beds were top of the line and the food was nutritious and she wouldn't have to worry about struggling in that broken-down RV of hers, well, it was more relief than I knew how to handle. "Do you think your mom would mind?" I asked, worrying about taking advantage of Rebecca's hospitality.

"Mind? She'll be ecstatic! And maybe the two of you could work together to build out the wellness side of the resort. She's mentioned Reiki and other woo-woo things like that in the past. Maybe that's something you're interested in, too?"

Lucas' words brought hope. Being near him brought hope. Knowing we were together brought hope. I leaned into him and he wrapped an arm around my shoulder. Together, we stared at the thin line where the ocean met sky and I dared to dream about the future.

CHAPTER THIRTY-EIGHT

C<small>AT</small>

As expected, the rest of the Huttons enthusiastically accepted the idea of moving Mom in to one of the bungalows. Rebecca and I talked about what Mom might need and if I had felt hope sitting on the beach with Lucas a few days ago, then I didn't have a name for what I felt when I finished talking with Rebecca. It was more than hope. It was almost...faith.

The day I went to talk to Mom, Lucas came with me. Conversation flowed between us until the Jeep rattled and bumped up to Mom's RV. She spun in her seat as two doors thumped closed and a slow smile brightened her face when she saw Lucas.

"Oh, Katydid. You told me he was gorgeous, but

you were holding back!" She extended a hand as Lucas let out a snort.

"Mom!" My cheeks burned bright and hot as Lucas shot me a glance filled with humor.

Mom's gaze locked on to mine and I knew she could tell I had something I wanted to say. "Don't bother trying to read my mind," I said. "I have every intention of explaining."

And explain I did as I launched into my spiel about Mom moving in at The Hut. She would be surrounded by people, with state of the art everything in terms of holistic healing. Yoga. Meditation. Massage. Food prepared by nutritionists with the simple goal of giving her body the nourishment it needed to put up a good fight. No one expected a miracle, but at least she would be comfortable. She protested, but not for long. Within minutes, she accepted the offer.

"If I'm honest, the thought of going through this again, alone, really lacks a certain appeal, you know?"

My knees went weak with relief. Moving Mom into The Hut felt so right, I had been prepared to fight her the rest of the week to make it happen.

Lucas shot a text to Rebecca, who promptly called back. He was close enough that I heard her first statement. "You know I don't text important information. Too easy to misinterpret." And then Lucas walked away, and her words were lost.

Mom drew me in for a hug. "I'm so happy for you," she whispered in my ear. "This man is perfect for you. I couldn't have asked for a better match."

I nuzzled close, breathing in her scent and trying to commit it to memory, suddenly not sure how long it would be until I forgot what she smelled like. That thought brought a lump to my throat and I pushed it away. Strength. Mom deserved my strength, not my sorrow.

Lucas returned with the news that Rebecca had a bungalow already set aside for Mom. "Whenever you're ready to make the move, we have a space for you."

Mom, in her way, declared there wasn't much reason to put it off. If the bungalow was ready, then so was she. And just like that, my mother had a private room at The Hut, her dilapidated RV looking tired and out of place in the parking lot.

By the time everything was said and done, night had fallen and exhaustion sat heavily on my shoulders. Lucas and I trudged upstairs, then stood by our respective doors, not ready to say goodnight.

"I can't believe all of this happened in the space of one day."

Lucas nodded but didn't respond, his eyes dark and distant. He was thinking something deep, something he probably would express beautifully if he could sit down and type it out. I wanted to press him to say what was on his mind, but didn't. Instead, I said "goodnight" and reached for my door.

"No," replied Lucas. "I want you with me." He grabbed my hand, swung open his door, and led me into his room, before wrapping me in an embrace that burned through the exhaustion I'd felt just moments before.

My body responded to his with a ferocity that surprised me. In a flurry of movement, we rid each other of our clothing and were on his bed, moving together.

Lost together.

Found together.

His skin. His touch. His taste. His smell. They were all answers to the question I hadn't known I had been asking for all of my life: *what have I been missing?*

As we moved, that still-small voice sighed in ecstasy, happy to finally have found what it was looking for.

Afterwards, we lay in a tangle of sheets and sweat, tired, but unable to sleep.

"What were you doing in Galveston?" I asked, aware that both of us had rooms at The Hut, that he didn't have a home he went back to at night.

"Nothing important. I've just been kind of floating

around since I got out of the hospital. This is the most grounded I've felt since before I got hurt."

"Because you're home?"

"Because of you." Lucas smiled as I made an incredulous face. "Okay, okay. Maybe also because I'm home."

"What happens when everything is settled here? Will you stay?"

"That's a good question. I thought I'd head back to Galveston to find a certain someone. But since I've already found her...maybe this is where I belong."

CHAPTER THIRTY-NINE

Lucas

Part of me hoped that Angela would recover. Part of me still believed in miracles. Part of me thought that we would bring her into the family, surround her with love and comfort, and the cancer would shrink away and she would thrive. In the months she lived with us, I grew to respect her vibrant humor, her adoration of her daughter, and her simple views on life.

The night she passed from this world was hard on all of us, but it devastated Cat. Angela managed to look her daughter in the eyes. A faint smile tugged at her lips and for the briefest of moments, the pain faded from her face. "Love him," she murmured in a voice barely above a whisper. "And through his love, learn to love yourself. You are everything I hoped you would be. I cherish you, Catherine. You are my greatest gift."

My heart swelled as Cat swallowed back her pain. "I love you, too, Momma," she said through a throat so thick it nearly strangled her words out of existence.

Angela closed her eyes and smiled, as if her daughter's love was stronger than any medicine, and as peacefully as a sigh of contentment, slipped away.

Cat cried until she couldn't breathe and I held her close, rubbing her back as her grief flowed.

Cat's dad flew in for the funeral and it quickly became evident that Dermot Wallace never stopped loving his wife. His grief-tightened features softened every time someone spoke her name and the number of times I caught him staring at Cat, cataloguing her features, grew too large to count. He was strong and stern and reminded me a lot of the early years with my dad— before the alcohol stole him from us.

After the service, we sat around the dinner table, nursing drinks while Dermot shared stories of the early years with his wife. He spoke of her beauty when he first saw her at high school—a wild child in a short dress with bright eyes and a flare for life. "For Angela, every day was special," he said. "Even if it was just a typical Monday filled with typical things, she would find a reason to celebrate. Maybe the sky was beautiful. Or the dinner was perfect. Or..." He shook his head and swallowed down the lump in his throat with a drink. "The world needs more people like her."

After that, he turned his attention to me, asking questions about my time in the Marines, my childhood, my future. Throughout it all, Cat sat quietly, her cool hand wrapped in mine. She smiled at his stories of her mother, and spoke when spoken to, but it was as if her light had dimmed. I stroked her thumb, careful to let her know I was there if she needed me.

"So, what's next for you, Lucas?" Dermot leaned forward, folding his arms on the table. "Sounds like things haven't really settled into anything permanent since you left the Marines. Are you staying in the Keys? Heading back to Texas? Something else?"

"I've been thinking a lot about that lately. Originally, I planned to stay here just long enough to help Mom and Wyatt get things in order and then find anywhere else to be. But now? There's more than enough work to keep me busy around The Hut and there's something really satisfying about coming home. Besides, with Cat here, I'm not ready to leave."

Dermot turned his attention to his daughter. "What about you, Catherine? You can't live in a hotel forever."

Cat glanced at her dad and sighed. "I don't know, Dad. I like it here. Lucas is here. And right now, I kind of just want to be wherever he is."

She leaned into me, resting her head on my shoulder as Dermot met my eyes. He smiled, even as sadness tugged at his features. "He's a good man. Anyone can see that. I'm sure he'll make sure you have everything you need."

"Lucas is everything I need," she replied and, in that moment, all the haze clouding my view of the future parted and I saw everything I wanted, for the rest of my life.

CHAPTER FORTY

CAT

Weeks turned into months and my grief passed. Missing Mom still felt like missing a limb. Like a basic part of me was gone, though sometimes I swore I could still feel her with me.

Lucas bought a house. An unassuming three bedroom near the water—not too far from The Hut. There was never any question as to whether or not I would move in. We just packed up our things and life entered a new phase, the two of us together, and stronger because of it. Eli and Caleb eventually went home, because for them, home wasn't that far away. They were still close enough to help out if they were needed, though between Lucas, Wyatt, and Rebecca they mostly had things sorted out. Wyatt carried more stress now than he did when I first arrived and Lucas said it was one last 'gift' from their father—an accounting error that went back for years. Harlow still had her room on the third floor, and no one really knew how long she intended to stay.

Rebecca and I worked together to understand everything we had learned about holistic healing during the time my mom spent at the resort. There were a million hotels stretched out along the Keys, but not many of them focused on the health and wellbeing of their customers. Together, we dreamed of a place people could come to stay and put their lives back together. A place of peace. Of health. Of joy.

Today had been a long day of training for me. One of the things that had brought my mom the most comfort was Reiki massage. I was determined to learn the intricacies so I could bring my clients that kind of relief—an homage to my mother. As I was washing my hands and gathering my things, my phone pinged with an incoming message and I was surprised to see Skywalker's old email address. We hadn't used those emails since we had learned the truth about each other.

from: Skywalker
<themanwhofoundyourjournal@imail.com>
   to: Katydid <getoveryourself@imail.com>
   date: March 14, 2019 at 5:39 pm
   subject: Miss me?

I've been reading all of our old emails, remembering how shocked I was to find your journal, almost as if you were left as a gift to me. It's easy to see how I fell in love with you, KatyCat, and as I was reading through your words, I realized how quickly and how deeply you had fallen for me.

   Maybe I chose not to act because I was blinded by the beauty of a charismatic redhead.

   Maybe I chose not to act because if I did, I would have to choose between the two of you and how could I do that?

   The person you keep hidden, the one you only showed me through our emails, she is so beautiful. You dad spoke of how your mom saw the magic in each day and I see that in you. You find something special in everything—maybe that's why you look at me like I'm some kind of miracle. You see something no one else has. Whatever the reason, I'm thankful for it. I'm addicted to the way you look at me. I crave it. Your love fills me up and spurs me on to become a better man.

With you, I feel whole again. There is no discon-
nect between what I think and what I say. I don't feel
the need to censor myself, nor do I feel the need to fill
the silence with idle chatter. I know you understand
and appreciate both sides of me and there is such
freedom in finally being myself.

Anyway, I'm rambling on.

By the way, you look so beautiful right now, I don't
know why I'm bothering to write an email when I
could just walk over and touch you...

When I looked up, I saw my Lucas, standing on the
back porch of The Hut, leaning against the rail. He
smiled as our eyes met and a surge of happiness
warmed my soul. That man, he was everything. I could
sum up my life in two distinct segments: pre-Lucas and
post-Lucas.

Before him, no matter how perfectly everything
went, no matter how hard I tried to find the beauty in a
given day, I was always aware I was missing something.
Even if I couldn't name it, even if I wasn't fully able to
understand the feeling, that still-small voice never
stopped whispering to me...

Find him.

And now that I had, now that I woke each morning

to his warm body stretched out next to mine, that quiet urging was gone. I was content. Maybe for the first time, ever.

I made my way across the sand to him, a question on my face. "What are you doing here?" I asked as I took the steps.

"I needed to see you and I couldn't wait for you to drive home." His gaze raked over my face, my body, and I swear, he saw straight through to my soul. "I am so in love with you."

"Well, now." I stepped closer, eager to be in his arms. "Doesn't that make me the luckiest woman in the world?"

Lucas regarded me as if I were the only thing on the planet worthy of his awareness. It was the look he gave me the first time I saw him, sitting behind the desk in the office. That first day, it unnerved me. It didn't anymore. I basked in the glow of his undivided attention.

Before I knew what was happening, Lucas lowered himself to one knee, holding out a small, black box with a dramatic diamond glittering in the setting sun. "I'm hoping you'll make me the luckiest man in the world. Will you marry me? Be my KatyCat for the rest of our years?"

In that moment, peace washed through me and I had the strongest sense of my mom—I inhaled deeply, imagining her scent traveling to me over the breeze. Tears pricked my eyes and I swallowed hard. "Oh, Lucas," I said, dropping down next to him. "I'm already yours for as long as the earth spins on its axis."

The backdoor swung open and Wyatt poked his head outside. "That means yes, right?"

I nodded, laughing, and Lucas helped me to my feet, then slipped the ring on my finger as the rest of the family filtered out, wrapping me in hugs and thumping Lucas on the back. He looked at me, a question in his eye.

"It's a yes," I murmured, and that still-small voice whispered *forever*.

EPILOGUE

Wᴡᴀᴛᴛ

Wow, Lucas and Cat! Who saw that coming? Answer
—all of us.

Watching the way they came together
reminded me of that feeling in your gut right
before a hurricane makes landfall—you could deny
it, you could protest it, you could get angry about
it, but the one thing you couldn't do, was anything
to stop it.

And good for them!

So what that they managed to stumble into that
rare, once-in-a-lifetime-if-you're-lucky kind of love that
most would kill for. That was no reason not to be
happy for them, even if it meant I had to force a smile

every time that happiness was all up in my face and I couldn't get away from it.

Which, considering one of them was an employee and the other was family, happened just about every day. So yeah, I had been pretty much screwed ever since they got together.

In my experience, ideas like love and relationships were highly overrated. In order to keep the hope of a magical happily ever after alive, no one ever thought about the negative side of love, especially not at the beginning when everything was new and beautiful. But for anything to be good, there must also be bad. How could there be yin without yang? How could one appreciate the light, if they had never seen the dark?

I witnessed that dark side firsthand—one more gift from my father. By the end, everything Burke Hutton touched turned dark. The only reason our family survived at all was because he died before he finished tearing us apart.

And even in that, shadows of him remained.

The most notable shadow of all?

Her.

Kara Lockhart. She had been a plague on my life, my heart, and my morality for years.

And after all we had been through...

...just when I thought I would never have to see her again...

...she came back.

———————

Thank you so much for reading Cat and Lucas' story. I hope you loved it as much as I did!

The Hutton family saga continues with Wyatt and Kara in Beyond Love. The quick with a smile, hardworking second son spent years battling his father's demons to win the love of his life and learn about the power of his own strength. I cried when I read the end of this book...let that sink in. Words I wrote, words I knew to expect, they moved me. I love Wyatt's story and I think you will, too.

I have a sneak peek for you on the next few pages, or

you can click or tap here to check out Beyond Love now!

Looking for signed books or more information on all things Abby Brooks? Check out my website!

www.abbybrooksfiction.com

BEYOND LOVE
SNEAK PEEK

PROLOGUE

Wyatt

My family knew our father was the villain in our story. What they didn't know was he had an accomplice.

Me.

Wyatt Hutton. The optimist. The man with a quick laugh and easy smile. The hard-working second son who sacrificed his wants and needs for the greater good of his family.

While that might have been true in the beginning, by the time my father was done with me, it was only a façade. I didn't just keep his secrets, I helped him bury them. I lied. I cheated. I stole. Under his guidance, I explored the darkest sides of my personality, and as much as they disgusted me, I didn't turn away. Instead,

I embraced them, then covered it all up and put on a brave face for everyone else.

Burke Hutton—the patriarch of our family, publicly beloved for his philanthropy, privately loathed for his alcoholism—had a mistress. A mistress with a taste for the decadent. A mistress with a daughter.

The girl wasn't my father's child, though it might have been better if she was.

Maybe things wouldn't have gone so far.

Maybe my dad would have gotten tired of the woman if it wasn't for the girl—a child he seemed to love more than his own flesh and blood.

Maybe I wouldn't have made so many mistakes if it wasn't for her.

Kara Lockhart. Innocent. Off-limits. And in desperate need of my protection.

She and I existed on the razor's edge of hate and love.

She was the biggest secret—and deepest regret—of my life.

I

THEN

CHAPTER ONE

Wyatt

Growing up, my dad's office was the most foreboding place in our home. Shrouded in shadows and stress, decorated with brooding masculinity and a firm, no-children policy, stepping over the threshold was akin to trespassing and punishable to the furthest extent of the law. As I aged and our home grew from a charming little bed and breakfast into a full-blown resort, I became a welcome asset in the room, but even now, as an adult, I found myself lingering in the doorway as if I needed permission to enter.

My father stood in front of the windows behind his desk, suitcoat draped over the back of his chair, shirt-sleeves rolled up to his elbows. Seemingly unaware of my presence, he sipped whisky as he stared at the ocean behind the house. Sunlight sliced through the window, catching in his salt and pepper hair and hiding his face in shadow.

It seemed a fitting metaphor.

Darkness overtaking light.

The father he had been devoured by the drunk he had become.

Massive furniture dominated the room. An imposing desk—dark wood and hard angles, with a towering, black leather chair hunkering behind it. Giant bookshelves covered in tomes I doubted he even read loomed against the walls. Mom tried to soften the room by adding plants and flowers, as if the pops of color and life could chase away the dark, but it didn't help. The darkness always won.

"Jesus, Wyatt. In or out." Dad sipped his drink, never taking his eyes off the window, his posture dripping disdain. No matter what choice I made, it would be the wrong one. If I stepped into his office, I would be the worst interruption of his day. If I backed away, he would see me as weak and therefore not worth his time in the first place.

The urge to flip him the bird, walk out the front door, and keep on going until I was somewhere else

—*anywhere* else—was strong. It had been for years. But as always, the thought of leaving Mom, Eli, and Harlow to deal with Dad kept me stuck where I was. I chose to stay for them, positioning myself as a buffer between the members of my family. If I left, they would have to deal with the asshole my father had become, and they deserved better than that. And so, I pushed those darker thoughts away and focused on my many reasons to smile—health, wealth, and a (mostly) happy family.

As I stepped over the threshold, Dad turned. "Take a seat." He indicated the chair across from his desk, then lowered himself into his own with a scowl.

Burke Hutton became predatory when he hung out with Jack Daniels. His actions weren't accidentally cruel. They were purposefully malicious. Crafted with the sole intention of targeting a weakness—one he had personally installed—and striking with enough force to knock me off balance. Over the years, I had learned to read his posture, the curl of his lips, the glint in his eye. His demeanor as he regarded me over his desk warned me to brace myself.

"At twenty-one, you're almost enough of a man to see the world for what it is. Cruel and hard." The way he narrowed his eyes made me wonder if he knew he was also describing himself. "Not the fairy tale world your mother lives in," he added, almost under his breath.

Mom's consistent optimism had once been a trait my father admired. As the years passed and his drinking increased, he grew to look down on her ability to find the good in anything. He claimed it made her weak. Vulnerable and easily taken advantage of. I often wondered if his anger stemmed from some awareness that he was the one taking advantage. It had to be easier to point his hatred outward instead of looking inward.

Dad cleared his throat, claiming my attention. "It's time for me to bring you in on a bit of a family secret."

Though, as he launched into his story, it became clear this wasn't a family secret.

This was his secret.

And it was terrible.

I listened in shock as my father told me about the mistress he had been supporting for the last three years. A mistress with a daughter—not his, thank God —and expensive taste. When he noticed the rage boiling beneath my surface, he paused long enough to laugh, a sound that buried bitterness in the pit of my stomach.

"You go right ahead and look all high and mighty now," he said as clouds covered the sun, casting a shadow over the room, "but wait a few years. Marriage is a prison sentence and men—*real* men—are built for freedom." He threw back the rest of his drink and spun the glass on the desk. "I'm dying a slow death with your mother."

"You're dying a slow death because you drink too much." My mother was a beautiful woman with a generous heart, someone who went out of her way to help people. She was too good for my father, and everyone knew it—even him, though he would never admit it.

Burke's eyebrows hit his hairline and I braced myself for his spiteful retort. Instead, he smirked and poured himself another glass. "The sooner the better then, right?"

There was probably a part of all of us that felt that way, though we wouldn't admit it. There was something awful in knowing hatred filled a heart that should be brimming with love. Instead, we made plans to scatter to the wind as soon as we were able, severing the very ties that kept us strong when we were young.

My older brother Lucas had been so desperate to get away, he joined the Marines the day he graduated from high school. My younger brother Caleb moved out the day he turned eighteen, supporting himself on a part-time fast food salary as he finished his senior year.

Eli counted the days until he could do the same. And poor Harlow had basically disappeared into herself, drawing and writing and playing the guitar as if she thought she could find a way to exist entirely in her own head.

While I was lost in thought, Dad continued to drone on about the mistress and her daughter—Madeline and Kara. I hoped he would get to the point quickly so I could decide what I was going to do with this knowledge.

"Man...that Kara..." Dad zeroed in on me, his gaze sharp as he catalogued my reaction. "That girl is something else. Sixteen. Smart. Talented. Good at everything she does." Those exact words could be used to describe Harlow, but Dad treated her like he would be happier if she didn't exist. His lip curled as he went in for the kill. "You could learn a lot from her. She's got more balls than you'll ever have."

She also, apparently, had private school tuition that needed paying. A luxury dad's biological children never had because, in his opinion, we needed a good dose of reality that only public school could provide.

"Why are you telling me this?" I asked, though I assumed he needed to clear his conscience. Dragging me down with him was just icing on the cake. I was part priest, part co-conspirator—absolving him of his sins as he implicated me in his crimes.

"As I get older"—Dad paused to take another drink —"it's going to get harder for me to hide these things. Especially the financial stuff. Your mom's too smart for her own good."

When he said *older*, he meant *more of a drunk*. "And you want me to help you hide it." The realization was a bucket of ice water poured over my head. I wasn't built for lies or deceit. Those things planted worry in my stomach and the roots dug painfully through my bones. Love and trust were meant to be honored, not thrown to the side like trash in the gutter.

"My son, ladies and gentlemen." Dad hefted his glass. "A Mensa candidate for sure."

I let the barb roll off me like water. Showing Dad he hit a sensitive spot only gave him a place to aim the next time and I was getting pretty good at laughing off his insults. "I won't do this," I said. "I can't lie to Mom. To my brothers and sister. This is your mess. You deal with it."

The man across from me had once been everything a boy could hope for in a father. Loving and kind. Willing to build his dreams out of sweat and hard work, and competent in teaching his children to do the same. Somewhere along the way, the alcohol burned that man out of existence, leaving nothing but a shell of the person I once admired. The intelligence that had allowed him to build The Hutton Hotel out of nothing but my mother's hopes and dreams was now allocated to finding new ways to torture his family and further his addictions.

"You have to do this." Dad glared at me, all joviality falling from his face. "If this secret comes out, it will destroy us. The whole damn family will fall to pieces, and you know as well as anyone that the family is the reason the hotel is so successful. If we go to shit, so does the business, and then what will we have? Nothing. No money. No credibility. We'd lose the house. Lose each other. We'd be done. That's why I chose you. Caleb's too weak, Eli's too dumb, Lucas is gone, and Harlow's head is filled with fluff. But you... you always do what's right." Dad lifted his glass. "Even when it's stupid."

An hour later, we pulled to a stop in front of a pretentious condo with manicured lawns, drooping palms, and a price tag so high, it made my head spin.

"What does Madeline do for a living?" I asked as I shut the car door behind me, swallowing a groan as the heat and humidity of the Florida Keys in July stole my breath. Saying her name felt dirty, like I was making room for her in my head and I really didn't want her there.

"Me." Dad smirked over his shoulder as he strode up the walk.

Great. So the mistress had expensive taste and no way to support it without dipping into my father's wallet. I took in the soaring architecture and pristine landscaping, trying to figure out the monthly rent, imagining dollar signs on everything I saw. "Let me guess. You pay for all of this."

The front door burst open as a bleached-blonde tornado siren came screeching into Dad's arms. "Burkey!" she squealed, her bright red lips cracking into a crocodile smile.

Dad grabbed the woman's breast and gave it a squeeze. "Paid for these, too," he said to me, while Madeline laughed and swatted at his hand. He flashed me a grin like a slap in the face.

Over the years, I thought I had come to terms with the man my father had become. That while he wasn't perfect, we'd all found a sense of equilibrium, making the best out of a bad thing. But standing on that sidewalk, watching him grope a woman who was not my mother, I realized there was nothing left of the man he used to be—of the man I secretly wished he would still be.

Madeline required an introduction, clearly unaware that Burke Hutton had kids. "Your son, huh?" She leered at me as thoughts ticked away behind cruel eyes. "It sure is a pleasure to get to know you," she purred, before calling over her shoulder, "Kara! Baby! Come here! There's someone you just have to meet!"

The last person I wanted to meet was the girl. I hadn't wanted to meet the mother, but that seemed a necessary evil as I would now be directly involved with helping her maintain her lifestyle. Meeting the girl—a child who made my father smile when I couldn't remember the last time any of his real family had managed that particular feat—felt like a step too far.

And the grin on Dad's face told me he agreed. Why did he take such pleasure in my discomfort? And for that matter, why did I care? He was a bitter old man intent on self-destruction. Instead of letting him drag me down, I focused on a drooping palm swaying in the breeze and the unending stretch of sky behind it until something, this sense of urgency, this *knowing*, demanded my attention.

Hey, the something whispered. *Look up. This is important. Look up. Now.*

"Well if it isn't Daddy Warbucks." Her voice wrapped around me like smoke, unusually deep for a female, almost rusty, and sexy as hell. It sent chills down my spine, and despite my best efforts to keep my gaze on the ground, I met her eyes.

She was young. Too young. Dark hair hung over delicate shoulders. Heart-shaped lips sat in a small face with large, gray eyes. Eyes that narrowed when they landed on mine.

"Wyatt Hutton," she murmured, half-prayer. Half-curse.

"Well, how did you know that when I didn't even know Burkey had kids?" Madeline squawked.

The glance the girl threw her mother's way was filled with enough disdain that even I caught it. "Because he talks about his kids sometimes? You never listen to anyone, do you?"

Burke pulled Kara in for a hug and my heart broke for my little sister. Harlow craved our father's approval like an addict craved her next fix, and here this Kara had him wrapped around her little finger. As Dad pressed a kiss into her hair, I caught a glimpse of the man he used to be. A man we all mourned, even though we still saw him every day.

In that moment, I hated Kara Lockhart. I hated her on behalf of my brothers and sister. I hated her on behalf of my mother. I hated her because my dad was right. If any of this got out, it would rip our family to pieces. I hated her because I knew I would keep his secret. And with that thought in my head, I realized I hated myself a little, too.

"Wyatt," Dad said when he released her, "meet Kara Lockhart. The daughter I should have had."

The more I knew about these people, the deeper I

would be pulled into Dad's secrets and lies, so I offered the girl a curt nod instead of a greeting and gave my attention to back to my feet.

CHAPTER TWO

Kara

Wyatt Hutton wouldn't look at me. Which was fine because when he did, it was like I was a piece of gum stuck to the bottom of his shoe. Like he couldn't believe he had to stand so close to a piece of trash like me.

Like I wasn't worth his time.

A flare of anger demanded I march right up to him and prove I didn't belong in the same box as my mother. The fact that he put me there without so much as a hello told me everything I needed to know about him.

He wasn't worth *my* time.

He was, however, much hotter in person than he was on Facebook. One of those people who didn't photograph well because his beauty was the kind that moved. I'd heard that line in a song once and never understood it until seeing Wyatt. But now, it made a magical kind of sense. Looking at him made me feel hopeful, which in turn made me feel ridiculous because it was clear he didn't like me.

He was tall—taller than I thought he would be. The resemblance to his dad was obvious, but also not immediately clear. Burke was like a redwood. Strong and sturdy. Thick arms, thick body, and thick legs. His personality took up massive amounts of space. Wyatt, on the other hand, was long-limbed. He had broad shoulders and a tapered waist. He was blonde where Burke was dark and smiled while Burke scowled. They were opposite sides of the coin, these men, though I wasn't sure what to do with that thought.

The most stunning thing about Wyatt was his eyes —even if I only saw them for a second before he refused to look at me again. They were such a light blue, they seemed to shine with a light of their own. For the heartbeat of time he deigned to favor me with his attention, they stole my breath.

I thought I would hate him. I thought I'd hate all of the Hutton kids, really. After all, they were living the life I would never have. They had two parents with stable jobs. They lived in a beautiful house that wasn't paid for with someone else's money. They were local royalty. Everyone knew the Hutton name, and no one had a bad thing to say about them.

The moment I looked at Wyatt, I realized I couldn't hate him—though it was obvious the feeling wasn't mutual. For as much as I thought he had the life I wanted, I had something of his, something he desperately craved.

His dad.

The image of the Huttons I had built by stalking their Facebook accounts was false. Their life was nowhere near the golden Utopia I daydreamed about. And how dumb did I have to be to ever think it was? I knew Burke was a cheat. I knew he was a drunk, too.

I guess I assumed that because he was so good to me, he was that good to everyone. That his own children knew him the way I did. Just five minutes of watching the way Burke treated his son blasted that idea out of the water. In fact, for a moment, I had an uncomfortable sense of kinship with Wyatt. He was a pawn for his father the same way I was a pawn for my mother. At best, we were tools they could use to further their own selfish endeavors. At worst...

...well, sometimes it was better not to think about the worst.

The days Mom couldn't drag herself out of bed and three-year-old me was left to figure out breakfast for herself. The oversharing of information, things no daughter should learn about her mother, as if we were best friends instead of flesh and blood.

As awkward as those days were, I much preferred them to the days where she had nothing but contempt for my existence. The days when simply seeing my face or hearing me move in my room brought her rage boiling to the surface. I spent so many years wondering what I'd done to make her hate me so much, but only recently realized that I hadn't done anything but take her attention away from the thing she valued most: herself. She resented me for the heinous act of being born. For weighing her down with responsibility and adding stretch marks to her belly and breasts. As if I had any say in the matter.

I had the uncomfortable realization that, in Wyatt's eyes, I wasn't all that much different from my mother. She was the other woman and I was the other child, both of us selfish enough to take time and attention from a man who wouldn't give it to his family.

And while I couldn't muster hate for Wyatt, I felt a heavy dose of resentment toward him. It wasn't like I chose this. It wasn't like I told my mom to sleep with a married man, then suck him dry for every spare dollar he would throw her way. I didn't ask for the fancy condo. Or the expensive car. It wasn't me who begged for the private school tuition, though I knew enough to value the education I was getting—it would be the key that set me free from this life.

I didn't ask to be born to a woman who was willing to sell her body to get what she wanted. I didn't ask to grow up without a father, without even an inkling as to who he was or what he looked like. I didn't ask to be my mother's keeper. And I certainly didn't ask for the way she kept looking from me to Wyatt and back again. She was hatching a plot with me at the center. I could see it in her eyes and whatever it was, I was sure to hate it.

I only had to survive this life for two more years and I would be free. Two more years until my eighteenth birthday, and I was out of here. I didn't have a clue where I would go, but at least I had the balls to look at my situation and know I had to get out. Wyatt couldn't even do that. He was five years older and still stuck at home, kowtowing to a man he obviously couldn't stand.

The little ball of hate I'd been building sputtered back to life. I glanced up, ready to eviscerate him with a single look, and my heart fluttered in protest when he met my gaze.

Despite myself, I smiled, which made him smile in return. It was a beautiful thing, warm and genuine and damn if hope didn't come rushing back to life, filling me with a sense of...of...the thought was gone before it could fully form. Wyatt looked away, rubbing a hand over his mouth and looking worried, and all the dark thoughts from before rushed back in to cover up that brief moment of light.

Confused, I said my goodbyes to Burke and retreated to the safety of my room.

Ready for more? Click or tap here to keep reading!

ACKNOWLEDGMENTS

So many people come together to bring my books into the world.

Thank you to my husband, my best friend, and my inspiration for all the perfect male characters. When I'm falling to pieces, you pick me up. When I'm flying too close to the sun, you keep me grounded. You are my sounding board, my confidant, and your arms feel like home. Thank you for the hours, days, and weeks you've spent with these words, helping me shape this story into what it needed to be. I love you with all that I am.

Thank you to my children. You guys make me feel like a superstar—even when I spend the day in my pajamas, staring like a madwoman at my laptop. I adore you.

Thank you to Joyce, Linda, Jackie, Nickiann, and Candy. Your feedback is everything I need. I appreciate your willingness to jump into a less than perfect book and give me your feedback. You guys are the best NotCheerleaders I could ask for and you mean so much to me.

To Zuul, Darlene, Hazel, Stormi, Elaine, Vanessa, Cynthia, and fleurtyfleur. Thank you for your support!

Books by

ABBY BROOKS

Brookside Romance

Wounded

Inevitably You

This Is Why

Along Comes Trouble

Come Home To Me

Wilde Boys Series with Will Wright

Taking What Is Mine

Claiming What Is Mine

Protecting What Is Mine

Defending What Is Mine

The Moore Family Series

Blown Away (Ian and Juliet)

Carried Away (James and Ellie)

Swept Away (Harry and Willow)

Break Away (Lilah and Cole)

Purely Wicked (Ashley & Jackson)

The London Sisters Series

Love Is Crazy (Dakota & Dominic)

Love Is Beautiful (Chelsea & Max)

Love Is Everything (Maya & Hudson)

Immortal Memories

Immortal Memories Part 1

Immortal Memories Part 2

As Wren Williams

Bad, Bad Prince

Woodsman

Connect with
ABBY BROOKS

WEBSITE:
www.abbybrooksfiction.com

FACEBOOK:
http://www.facebook.com/abbybrooksauthor

FACEBOOK FAN GROUP:
https://www.facebook.com/
groups/AbbyBrooksBooks/

TWITTER:
http://www.twitter.com/xo_abbybrooks

INSTAGRAM:
http://www.instagram.com/xo_abbybrooks

BOOK+MAIN BITES:
https://bookandmainbites.com/abbybrooks

Want to be one of the first to know about new releases, get exclusive content, and exciting giveaways? Sign up for my newsletter on my website:

www.abbybrooksfiction.com

And, as always, feel free to send me an email at: abby@abbybrooksfiction.com

Made in the
USA
Middletown, DE